THE WORLD WITHOUT A FUTURE

Book One of World Without End

By
Nazarea Andrews

The World Without A Future by Nazarea Andrews
All rights reserved. Published in the United States of America by A&A Literary.

Summary: 20 years after the zombie apocalypse, two unlikely allies struggle to survive when their town is overrun by the undead.

978-0-9894799-2-9

1. Romance. 2.Zombie. 3. New Adult.

For information, address 14207 Ridge Court, Upatoi GA 31829.
www.nazareaandrews.com

Edited by Rachel Bateman
Cover design by Melissa Stevens of The Illustrated Author
 Cover art copyright©: Nazarea Andrews
Ebook Formatting by Ink in Motion
Paperback Formatting by Ink in Motion

Books by Nazarea Andrews

After the Fall Series:

Edge of the Falls

Chasing the Wind (March 2014)

University of Branton:

This Love

Beautiful Broken

Sweet Ruin (April 2014)

World Without End:

The World Without A Future

with AJ Elmore

Prince of Blood and Steel (January 2014)

Nazarea Andrews

Dedication

The three ladies I couldn't do without, and
The ones who loved this world first:
Chanteé, Bri, and Jess.
Hugs and chocolate for all of you!!

Nazarea Andrews

THE WORLD WITHOUT A FUTURE

Book One of World Without End

By
Nazarea Andrews

Table of Contents
Part 1

Part 2

Nazarea Andrews

Part 1

The Girl Without a Birthday

*

We know we're getting old when the only thing we want
for our birthday is not to be reminded of it.

~Author Unknown

**

The children born the Day of Death will be the
key to our salvation.
Their death will bring new life to our world.
From The Writings of the High Priest

Nazarea Andrews

Chapter 1

Phantoms of a Dead World

I was born the day the world died.

Sometimes, when my brother—he's all I have left—talks about that time, I wish I had been alive for it. I wish I had seen it—shopping malls, grocery stores, even playgrounds without razor wire fencing and armed guards.

Then again, I don't always believe him. Who the hell goes somewhere open and exposed without some visible protection?

I think the ones who were born after the change were lucky. We don't know enough to miss the old life. We didn't lose anything. We've always had the infects, the razor wire and guns, the drills. We've always lived behind walls.

Sometimes, I'll see Collin watching the horizon, watching the clouds scuttling over the walls, and I know he misses it—the freedom of travel, of life without our fences. And I'll pity him, a little. Because he is old enough to know exactly what was lost twenty years ago.

The day that I was born.

Chapter 2

Early Mornings in Hellspawn

I wake up to warmth, an arm thrown over my hips, pulling me into him. I smile, a happy little movement. It's still new, this thing between Dustin and me. New enough that waking up next to him is a little bit thrilling. I snuggle closer to him and feel his lips curve against my neck. "You're awake," he says, drawing me to him. He shifts, so I'm pinned under him as he grins down at me.

Dustin. The best friend I've known my whole life—or long enough that nothing else matters. He came to the Hive when his parents were relocated to Hellspawn—Haven 8, to the rest of the world. Walked with me to and from our daily classes. Protected me from the bullies and new Walkers looking to make an impression.

He was the big brother whenever Collin wasn't around. He was with me when Collin Walked the wall for the first time.

And he kept me safe, kept my name and what I was quiet.

He leans down and kisses me, and I arch up to meet it. It still shocks me, the first brush of soft lips, the intensity that builds up beneath it, the fact that the hands that have cradled and helped me are holding me again, differently. Warming and gentle as he strokes over my arm and eases my sleep top down. Outside the tiny window, I can hear the low clang of the church bell.

"Stop," I murmur, catching his hand as it slips under my shirt. "Collin is on his way."

Resignation flickers across his face, and he nods. "I should get dressed."

I prop myself up and watch as he crawls from bed, his smooth, unscarred chest rippling with motion. I grin, and he smirks at me. "See something you like?"

I shrug. "Maybe."

He laughs and leans down to kiss me. Beyond the thin cloth barrier, I hear keys in the front door and the tumble of the locks being slid back. Dustin winks and slides out of my tiny room.

There's a frozen moment as the door opens and my brother and Dustin face off. Then, a low, softly accented voice mutters, "Get out of the way, Collin."

My lips curl in disgust. Of course he's here. He seems attached at the bloody hip to Collin these days.

My brother's voice, deep and steady and reminiscent of everything safe, fills the small apartment. "You should head home, Finn."

The air goes still, and I hold my breath. Danger changes the way the air feels, the way it moves around you. It feels charged, somehow. I feel it during a breech, when zombies swarm sections of the Haven. I feel it again, now.

Then I hear heavy footsteps and Dustin releasing the breath he's been holding.

"Is she asleep?" Collin asks.

"Yes."

"I like you, Dustin. You've been good to Ren—protected her as much as you can and been a solid friend."

"Thank you, sir. I try."

"How long has this been going on?"

Dustin shifts, clears his throat. I grin—he's intimidated by my tall, quiet brother. Always has been. "Long enough."

I hear Collin sigh and drop his bag on the table, the blades inside clattering noisily. "I can't stop this—and don't even want to. But have a little discretion, huh? She's my baby sister."

I flush, but lie quiet and still. Dustin mumbles something, and Collin steps over to the door. "She'll meet you downstairs for work duty. Go on."

The door clangs shut, and Collin sighs again. I should have told him about this—about the night at the track three weeks ago, when Becks said something nasty and rude to me and Dustin pulled me back before I punched her. About him dragging me down the beaten dirt path and calming me down, and me leaning up and kissing him, a kiss fueled by aggression and liquor and the simmering attraction that had been getting harder and harder to ignore.

I didn't though, because Collin didn't have anyone—hadn't had a woman in his life since before he Walked the wall. The only people who mattered to Collin were me and his best friend.

I step out of my curtained bedroom when Collin calls me for the fifth time. He's glaring at his watch and points abruptly at my breakfast. A mushy apple and a piece of stale toast. Ration day is still two days away, and we're scraping the bottom of the barrel. Because Collin gave the orphans next door some of our rations. Again. I toss the apple at him wordlessly, grab my bag off the floor, and head for the door.

"Where's your gun?" Collin calls out.

I stop, lifting my work shirt to expose the snub-nose revolver tucked into a holster on my hip. It's my favorite, because Collin gave it to me, when I turned ten. That was the year Mom died. "And I have my 9mm in my bag. And my knife in my boot," I say.

That's his rule. Three weapons any time I leave the house. And four back up rounds of ammo.

We haven't had a breach in Haven 8 in six months. The last one was in sector four, down by the tracks. Completely other side of Hellspawn. But Collin never lets up—every morning when he stumbles in from Walking, before I leave for work, he checks my weapons.

I guess if I watched everyone I knew die, I'd be super careful with my baby sister too.

Collin follows me to the door, leaning against the wall as I begin to undo the locks. "What do you want for your birthday?"

It's that time of year again, and I bite my tongue on my answer. *A party.* A real one, with cake and laughing, music and dancing, presents. A party where people aren't looking morose and crying and talking about that day twenty years ago, when everything changed. A party not tainted by mourning, incense, and the screams from the Order's victims.

I don't say that, because a party isn't possible—not for me. Not on Day One. So I shrug and try to look like it's not a big deal, even though Collin sees through me, and always has. "A new bag would be good—this one is getting ratty," I say, holding up the bag I've been carrying since he handed it down to me.

His eyes narrow, assessing me, and I grin at him. He's not buying it, but I just need to get out the door. By tonight, he'll be too tired to ask me about my birthday. Or Dustin. We're both pretending that didn't happen, which I'm perfectly okay with.

He opens his mouth to say something, but I step out, yelling, "Bye, stay safe!" I let the door slam shut on his words and dart into the wide open hallway.

Collin hates living in the complex. He says that during the change, they were deathtraps, whole floors being changed and spilling out on the next until the entire complex was one hungry infection. Narrow hallways and no way out made for a chute of death that left no one alive.

That was at first. It took a while, once the change hit, for the survivors to learn how to fight back. How to survive.

"Nurrin!"

My name ringing through the hallway jerks me from my musings, and I whip around to glare at Dustin. "What the hell did I say about that name?"

He grins at me, wrapping a thick arm around my shoulders and squeezing me into his side. "Sorry, Ren. But you weren't answering." He frowns down at me, and I flush. "You okay?"

I pull away, adjusting my bag, and nod. "I'm fine. Let's go."

Dustin opens his mouth. And closes it again. Smart boy, he is. Then again, he's been with me long enough that he *should* know when not to push.

I slam out of the Hive, and I'm immediately stopped, a tiny red laser dot painted on my chest.

"Slow the fuck down, Ren," Billy growls. I flip him the bird as Dustin drags me away.

"Biters, girl, what the hell is wrong with you?" he mutters as I amble after him in the street. It's clogged with workers headed to the orchards, parents to the factory, soldiers coming off shift on the wall. All of us moving at a glacial pace because moving too fast would be *distressing*. "Are you upset about Collin catching us this morning?"

I don't want to answer him—he's annoyed enough, and if I do answer, he'll just think I'm being moody. I chew on my lip and ignore the question. "No. I'm just tired—and hungry. Rations are low."

Dustin changes the subject. "Do you think we'll be in the apples today?"

I shake my head. "Cherries. Kelly said they finished the apples last week."

Everyone in Hellspawn works the orchards or fields, twice a week. It keeps us fed without devoting half the Haven's population to it. It's boring work, and I would rather be on the wall, but

I have another year before I'm allowed to even apply for training.

Even then, I have to have a secured sponsor. Collin works the wall, but he'd never go for me up there. The only friend he has on it is Finn.

And I'd rather walk naked and unarmed a mile from the wall than ask Finn O'Malley for a damn thing.

Chapter 3

The Bells Toll

I was right. We work the cherry trees, which puts me at the top of a tree, picking fruit from the fragile branches and praying I don't fall, while Dustin stands on a ladder, filling buckets from the lower, thick branches and laughing with the girls who come to take our crop.

I swallow another curse as I hear Becks Lawson laughing at something Dustin says. I zip my pouch full of cherries closed and swing down, so quick I almost lose my grip a few times, scurrying faster than a squirrel.

"Biters, Ren," Dustin says, when I'm a few branches above him. "You need to be careful."

I throw the pouch at him. "Hurry up."

He unzips the bag, and, even from here, I can see him pale. His head snaps up as he drops it like it's on fire. Becks screams, a little, and I'm suddenly conscious of the blood on my palms and the speed I'm moving at.

Both signs of infection.

Dustin whips around, clamping a hand over Becks mouth before she can scream it, and I'm so relieved I'm dizzy. I'm not infected—I can't be, I haven't been exposed to an infect in over six months. Not since before the last breach. I'm *clean*, dammit.

"She's clean," he's whispering, "There's not a damn thing wrong. Do you want to spend a week in Q because she scraped her hand on the tree?"

Becks looks at me, her eyes wild above his hand, and I slide down the tree. Dustin glances back at me, and I slow my movements, making them exaggeratedly slow. I hold up my hand—it's raw, but bark is stuck in it. "I'm clean," I say, my voice deliberately loud and clear.

At the third sign, Becks sags with relief, and a choked sob breaks from her. As soon as Dustin lets her go, she snatches up the cherries and gets away from us as fast as she can without arousing suspicion.

Three signs—the trinity of infects that we were taught in pre-school. Before the change, kids learned their colors, their letters, and how to draw circles. Now no one gives a damn about color except that it draws the attention of infects. Letters are still important, and so are circles— hitting one dead center. After the change, we learned that infects move fast—almost inhumanly fast. They are constantly bleeding, a byproduct of the infection and the decay of their own bodies. And they can't speak—not clearly.

It's why open wounds are taboo, why everyone over-enunciates, and why running in Hellspawn is prohibited anywhere but the three mile track on the east side.

I drop to my knees, suddenly dizzy and weak with relief. Dustin crouches next to me, a hand on my shoulder steadying me. "Change above, Ren, you have to be careful," he admonishes, his voice low and angry.

I look up, miserable. "It's almost my birthday, Dustin."

He rocks back on his heels, and understanding flickers in his eyes for a second. "That's why you're so jumpy."

I look away. Open my mouth to say something—I'm not sure what. And above us, the alarm begins, the screaming bells. All the blood rushes from my face, and I jerk to my feet.

"It's a breach."

Chapter 4

The Hive

"You can't," Dustin snaps at me as I push through the throng of students headed for the nearby Hatch. I ignore him. Only one thought consumes me—there's a breach, and Collin is alone.

Nothing else matters—not the infects that will kill me if they catch me, not the rules saying I should be headed to the orchard Hatch, not even Dustin steadily cursing as he follows me. Just my brother.

Collin sleeps to music—he always has. And that will drown out the bells tolling through Hellspawn. Terror grips me as I think about that, about Collin alone and unaware of the threat. I break into a sprint, and around me, my peers scatter, screaming. I almost expect to be shot, but someone appears at my side, keeping pace with alarming ease.

I want to tell him to go away, but I don't have the breath to bother, and I'm more interested in getting to Collin. Besides, Finn never does what I tell him to. And no one will shoot at me, not with a Wall Walker racing along at my side, in full uniform and heavily armed.

"How many rounds do you have?" he demands.

"Four. Two guns. A knife," I snap out and push on more speed as the bells scream out their warning. Where the hell are they?

From the corner of my eye, I see one. It's racing through the orchard, skin flapping behind it. Its mouth is gaping open, teeth bloody. A girl—a little blonde—darts from behind a tree, and the zombie screeches, tackling her. I gag, forcing myself to move faster. Finn is cursing, and I'm suddenly aware that I've lost Dustin, and then the Hive appears, and there's no one near it. No infects, no guards, nothing. It's a massive, steel and stone structure that seems impossibly untouched. I sob, staggering, and Finn catches me, jerking me through the stairs door.

I'm up the stairs and fumbling for my keys, my ears ringing from the continuous noise. Finn almost vibrates with impatience. He snatches the keys from me, quickly unlocking the door, and we tumble into the apartment.

"Get whatever you need. We won't be back," Finn orders as he strides to Collin's bedroom, yanking the curtain open. I look away quickly—Collin sleeps naked, and that's more brother than I have any desire to see.

"Get up," Finn orders, yanking the ear buds from Collin's ear. He jerks awake with a suddenness that makes me nervous, a gun appearing in his hand. Finn knocks it aside. "There's been a breach."

"How many?" Collin demands, reaching for a pair of pants. I relax when I hear the button snap.

"A horde. I've never seen that many infects in one place," Finn says, his voice low and grim.

"Ren!" Collin shouts, and I jerk, wondering how he knew I'd be here. Finn is in the kitchen, shoving what little food we have left into a bag when I emerge.

"What?" I snap, and the sirens go silent. As scared as I was before, it's nothing compared to the silence. I look nervously at my brother and his best friend. "What happened?"

"You ready to go?" Collin asks instead, and I shake my head. "Where are we going?"

Finn is suddenly in front of me, his eyes hard, and I flinch away from them, and his words. "Hellspawn is falling, Ren. A horde of roughly five hundred zombies just overwhelmed the east wall. If the siren is off, there's no one left alive over there. We're about to be overrun. We need to get out. Now."

I send a terrified glance to Collin, but he doesn't say anything to dispute it. His expression is resigned. I close my eyes and nod. "Five minutes."

"One." Finn answers, and I move.

Chapter 5

The Horde

It hits me when we're on the stairs, and I come to a complete stop. "I can't leave Dustin," I say, my voice a whisper, but my words vehement.

Finn glances up at me then shakes his head, letting Collin handle this. My grip tightens a little on my gun, and I want to point it at Finn's head and pull the trigger. Stupid ass.

"Where did you last see him?"

"He was following me. I was in the orchard, and I had to get back here. Finn found me, and I lost him."

For the first time, I wonder what the hell Finn had been doing—he walks the south wall, the most dangerous perimeter. What was he doing in the orchards?

"If we see him, we'll take him with us," Collin says, and I hear Finn's soft snort of disgust ahead of us in the darkness. I aim a kick at his leg, and he moves lithely away. "Stop it, both of you." Collin's voice is tight and angry, laced with worry.

It makes both of us stop immediately. "The horde was on the east wall," Finn says.

"So we head west." I say, reasonably, and Finn gives me a look I can't decipher.

"I have two vehicles on the west side."

Something in his voice makes me look at him. "You won't like them," he says, quietly, to my brother.

I mutter a curse, and Collin snaps his fingers in front of my face. We're at the exit to the Hive. There's no noise outside, nothing that hints at any horde—nothing that hints at life. "You ready?" my brother asks, and I nod. There's not really a choice. "Stay between us. We'll cover you.," he says, and Finn steps up to flank me. I don't trust him, but Collin does, and that counts for something.

Then Collin eases the door open, and Finn bursts through it. In the distance, I can hear screams. For a heartbeat, they root me in place. Then Collin shoves me, and I break into a sprint, chasing Finn.

We're two blocks from the Hive when I hear the first footsteps behind us, and I dart a glance over my shoulder. Three infects, racing after us. Before the change, people assumed zombies were slow. I've seen the videos, the movies about the shambling dead. But something about ERI-Milan gave them a surplus of adrenaline and speed that a human can't match. We can beat them at a sprint, but an uninfected human gets tired. The adrenaline wears off. Now the zombies race through Hellspawn, and evidence of the breach is everywhere. The screams, the scent of blood and decay thick in the air, the blood beginning to spread on the stone pathway.

"Collin!" I shout. He nods, and Finn flips around, running backward as he pulls his small crossbow. I hear a soft whir and a body falling. The snarls are louder, closer, and Finn fires again, quickly.

Then he's turned back and catches my arm—when did I slow down?—pulling me up alongside Collin.

"WAIT!"

The voice stops me cold, skidding around to stare in hopeful disbelief as Dustin breaks from a little shop. He's covered in blood and is limping. "Dustin!" I shout, taking a half step toward him. Finn grabs me and jerks me to a stop.

"Collin, five coming at you," Finn says, his voice urgent. My brother shoots, but I can barely see anything but my best friend limping toward me. I grab him, pulling him into me, searching him frantically for bites. He's bloody, and his face is twisted in pain. But he isn't bitten. That's the most important thing.

"How?" I start, but Finn is pulling me on, and Dustin struggles to keep up, limping as he does.

"Question him later. Did you miss the part where a horde invaded Haven? We need to get the fuck out. *NOW.*"

I hate that he's right. "We aren't moving fast enough," Collin pants, and I look around. Zombies are headed toward us at full speed, and we've slowed down to accommodate Dustin's limping gait.

Finn looks around, and I glance at him. "Will we make it?" I ask, my voice low enough that Dustin won't hear me. His jaw is tight, and his eyes are angry.

"Go. Collin, you know where. Get her safe." He's stopped, unclipping his guns. I look at him, stunned, and then to Collin.

"No. No freaking way. You can't hold an entire horde off."

Finn flashes me a dangerous smile, one that screams confidence and disdain. "Didn't think you gave a damn."

"I don't," I snap, flushing. Unfreakingbelivable. I'm embarrassed in the middle of a breach.

Finn reaches for me, and I jerk back, startled. His fingers graze my hair, and something fills his eyes for a heartbeat. "Go. It's not far. I can hold them long enough."

Collin doesn't hesitate—he yanks me back into motion, and I'm too stunned to protest when we round a corner and Finn disappears.

Chapter 6

Buying Time

He was right. The cramped storage unit where his cars are isn't far—four blocks away from where we abandoned Finn. Collin isn't saying anything, but I can see his hands shaking as he yanks the door open with a rattle. The noise echoes, and Dustin flinches. "Get in," Collin orders, and I help Dustin into the sleek little car nestled under the blue tarp. As I peer into it, I go very still then straighten.

"Collin. This car only seats two."

"I know," he says. "Finn planned for this. You and I were supposed to be in the car, and he'd ride the bike to cover us."

The bike he reveals is tiny, sleek, and, instinctively, I know it's fast. And a thought occurs to me. "Collin, you drive Dustin. I won't be able to avoid the infects in that—I can dodge better on the bike."

My brother pauses in the middle of gathering weapons and looks at me. "You can't go back for him."

I laugh out loud. "What on earth makes you think I *want* to go back for Finn O'Malley?"

Collin stares at me for a moment longer, and I meet his gaze head on. And then he nods. "Ok. Come on, let's get you in some gear."

Five minutes later, I'm dressed in skin-tight, bite-resistant armor, a gun in the top of both my boots and several knives attached to the bike itself. I feel like a walking armory. Collin looks at me. "Was Dustin bitten?"

I look at my boyfriend. He's tense—his whole body taut and anxious—but his eyes are closed, as if he's sleeping. "No. I think he got caught up in the crowd—and I think the ankle is broken."

Collin nods. We can hear the sound of gunfire, footsteps and screams, drawing closer. He kisses me quickly on the forehead. "Stay safe. And close. We'll need to move fast when we get past the walls."

I nod and, Collin's gaze darts past me. Finn still hasn't appeared. And we're out of time.

Chapter 7

Escape from Haven 8

The Porsche 911 is quiet—almost soundless—as it prowls onto the eerily empty street, and I follow with the soft purr of the crotch rocket.

I can hear the screams, the sound of fighting, and the wet rip of flesh as zombies feast—the citizens of Hellspawn are buying us time. The zombies are too intent on feeding to notice us slipping away two streets down. Collin steers quickly, toward the west wall, toward the promise of open roads to escape the horde. I watch him from behind my helmet. It's coming up, the tight little alley I saw. He won't be able to turn around there. My whole body is tight with nerves and anticipation. He turns, and the Porsche eases down the alley. I hit the gas, the bike jumping forward.

Leaving my brother behind.

Finding Finn shouldn't be hard—all I have to do is follow the trail of dead infects. And leaving him...I shake my head. Even as much as I dislike Finn, I can't abandon him to a horde. No one deserves that.

I ease the bike up to a corner and peer around. The trail of dead led here. A lone shot rings out, and a body falls. The other infects are snarling, a vicious song of hunger and hatred as they dart back and forth.

I peek around the corner and see them. Ten infects gathered around a low overhang. Finn's perched there. As I watch, he lines up another shot, and his gaze lands on mine.

Shock and something else—hope?—fills his eyes for an instant before anger flares, taking over.

He *would* be furious.

I push that thought aside—along with the strange emotions I keep seeing—and aim. All I have to do is clear a path.

I get three shots off before the infects realize I'm there. As they turn, Finn shouts, and four quick shots ring. Three more bodies drop, but the remaining four are converging on me. I shoot two, and the others are on me. I can hear the pound of feet, and it occurs to me as one of the biters snaps at my arm, this was a stupid idea, and then blood sprays, and I swallow a scream as the zombie's head goes spinning. Finn is glaring at me over the bloody steel of his sword, and I manage to swallow as he demands, "Did it bite you?"

"No."

"Scoot back, Ren. I'm not riding bitch on my own bike."

He shoves me a little, and I slide back, letting him swing onto the bike. It rumbles under him, and he shouts, "Hang on," and I plaster myself to him.

And then we're racing through the streets, and if the infects realize we're here, they don't have a chance in hell of catching us. I can see the west wall, rising a hundred feet up, twenty feet thick, and I wonder where his exit is. In a breach, all the gates will be locked down.

He swings us to the south, and I can see the Porsche skidding through blood and gore—how the hell did the infects get this far into Haven so quickly?

Finn curses and gives the bike a little more speed. I stifle a scream as we lurch forward. A grate—low and dark—is open, and he angles for it. Collin flashes his lights twice, and Finn waves back. Then we're swallowed up by darkness.

Chapter 8

The Wide Open

We burst out of the tunnel into light so brilliant, I'm not sure how Finn can see. He's still cursing, a soft, steady stream of noise that rings in my ears. Behind us, Collin keeps pace in the Porsche.

And that's when it hits me and I pull away from Finn a little, shock slamming into me. His hand clamps down on my wrist, jerking me back against him. I know what he'd say, if I could hear him. *Keep your shit together, Ren.*

But how? We're in the freakin' Wide Open, the massive stretches of unsettled land that belong to the infection, the stretches between Havens that are teaming with zombies. The only thing that kept us safe was the walls around our cities, and we're not behind them anymore—and even if we were, the zombies are there as well. A scream bubbles in my throat, aching for an escape.

Strangely, it's Finn who steadies me.

I've hated Finn since I met him, three years ago. It was a week after Collin was sponsored to the wall, and I came home from school to find my brother and Finn sitting on the couch, bags of melting ice on their faces. I knew who he was— Hellspawn wasn't so big that I could miss Finn O'Malley. But I'd never spoken to him.

Finn was different. He came to Haven instead of being born here, and he was an orphan—but then, many of us were. But where Dustin and Becca and others bonded with me and Collin, forming loose families within the Hive, Finn wanted none of it. He seemed to enjoy the distance and solitude.

I'd never heard of the wealthy orphan having friends. Until that day he punched my brother and got both of them sentenced to extra walks for a month—and docked rations.

After that day, he never left. Not really. And I hated him, for sharing something with Collin that I couldn't, and for hitting my brother, and for thinking he was too good for the rest of Haven. The girls in the Hive fluttered like idiots when he dropped by, something Finn was very aware of.

I couldn't stand him, and the dislike was reciprocated. That I had saved his life—well, that had everything to do with him saving all of ours.

"Nurrin, infects are coming," he shouts, over the roar of the wind

I glance back and see them—three older infects. The females are oozing blood, hideously disfigured in their semi-naked state. One's arm is twisted back at an unnatural angle that hurts just to look at. The male lopes along behind them, his jaw unhinged and hanging open.

"Take my gun," Finn orders, and I obey, pulling it from between us. He slows down, and I fight the terror that grips me as I realize he's letting them gain on us. I push that thought aside—he thinks I can do this. And Finn isn't so self-sacrificing he'd risk his life twice.

The thought clears my head, and I squeeze the trigger. The first infect drops, blood spraying up in the face of her pack mates. Three more squeezes and the others are dead.

Truly dead, not the half-there sate they'd been suspended in. Killing isn't fun—but there's something soothing about giving them that final shot, the final bit of rest.

And if I didn't, they'd just tail us back to— where the hell are we *going?*

I tuck the gun into Finn's holster and lean closer to ask, but he revs the engine, and we race across the Wide Open in a roar of wind that steals all conversation.

Chapter 9

Suicide Wish

Darkness has begun to fall when I feel the bike slow. The Porsche prowls behind me. We haven't stopped today, except for once, refueling the vehicles from a cache of gasoline Finn had hidden in a graveyard.

The bike cuts off, and I shiver in the soundless twilight. We're near the edge of a cliff—the Grand Canyon. I almost fall off the bike, and Finn catches me, righting me with barely restrained violence. I pull away from him as Collin explodes from the car. It's the first time I've seen him—he didn't get out of the car when we stopped for fuel. Finn's orders, and it was incredibly chafing that my brother listened to him.

"Ren, are you okay?" he demands, sweeping me into a hug. It's a stupid question. If I had been bitten back in Haven, risking my ass for Finn, I'd have changed hours ago. But his concern is touching, mostly because it means he's not pissed. Not pissed is good.

"I'm fine, Collin," I say, pulling away. He lets me go and frowns at me, then over at Finn.

"You're a fucking idiot, is what you are," Finn snarls, and I flinch away from the venom in his voice and the words themselves.

Then anger fills me, and I shove him. "I saved your ass, you bastard!"

"You exposed yourself in a breach. You were unarmed, with no means of escape and on even ground. I know Collin's taught you better, so tell me, Nurrin, do you *have* a death wish?"

"I was armed, and I saved you!" I scream.

"You took an unneeded risk!"

I open my mouth to tell him to go fuck himself, and behind us, Dustin shouts, "Will someone get me *out* of here? I have to pee and I'd like to be part of this yell-at-Ren moment."

Finn's eyes flick past me, and disgust fills his expression for a heartbeat. His gaze skates to Collin. "He's her baggage. I'm not taking care of it."

Collin's lips compress a little, but that's the only sign of his irritation. Finn turns away from me, and I grab his arm, still spoiling for a fight. He gives me a bored look. "I'd like to get to the Hole before the infects show up, Nurrin. Do you mind?"

"Take care of Dustin," Collin asks. "It'll be a few minutes before we're ready."

Fuming, I turn to help my friend out of his seat. Blood loss has turned his skin clammy and pale, and I freeze for a moment, not wanting to touch him. Years of being told bleeding is a sign of infection makes approaching him now difficult—bordering on impossible.

He summons a weak smile. "Help me up, Ren. I really do have to piss."

I roll my eyes and reach for him, avoiding the blood on his sleeve. "You should have headed to the Hatch, idiot."

"And then what? When we thought it was safe and came out—what then?"

I go still, staring at him with wide eyes. His gaze is bitter and filled with grief, and it hits me suddenly—I fall to my knees with a low cry. Finn catches me, jerking me away from Dustin, crushing me to his chest. I feel his tension, and I know he's drawn a gun on my best friend, and I can't hold back the wail of grief building in my throat.

"Did he hurt you?" Finn demands, his voice harsh. I shake my head against his chest, and some of the tension eases out of him as he pulls me away to look into my eyes. His gaze softens, just a little. "The Haven?"

I nod, hating that he's seeing me this weak. Finn's eyes shutter, and he releases me. "Go. Fall apart when we're safe."

Dustin catches me as I stumble away, and we lean against each other as we follow Collin and Finn toward the edge of the cliff. For a moment, staring off the cliff, I wonder where the hell we're going. Finn looks at Collin. "Take point. Dustin behind you, then Nurrin. I'll bring up the rear."

Collin glances at me then nods, scooping a bag off the pebbly, hard ground. Then he steps forward. The path—if it can be called that, and really, it shouldn't—is so narrow, I'm not sure how he finds footing on it.

I have no idea how Dustin will. He hesitates for a moment, and from behind me comes Finn's voice, sharp in my ear. "You go down, or stay here, but get the fuck out of the way, dude."

I turn to glare at him, but he's staring at Dustin, his expression bleak. Dustin grinds his teeth audibly behind me and follows my brother down the cliff side.

"Take this," Finn says, handing me the bag. It takes me a moment to adjust to the weight of it, and I can feel Finn's gaze on me, avid and assessing. I straighten and turn away, stepping onto the path.

And ignore the half smirk that turns Finn's lips.

Chapter 10

The Hole

"What is this place?" I ask, my awe apparent in my voice. Finn steps past me, his body brushing against my arm. I step away, quickly, moving to Dustin.

"I call it the Hole. My parents set it up a few years after the fall. It was always a safe place for us to fall back."

It's the most revealing thing Finn has ever said, and I look at Collin—he doesn't seem surprised. He doesn't seem even startled by the electricity pumping through the cave; the comfortable, if dusty looking furniture; and the little kitchen in the back, open cabinets stocked with MREs and canned goods.

He's been here before. Finn has shared this with him, and Collin never mentioned it. Anger flares in me, and I turn to Dustin, kneeling in front of him on the couch and yanking at his boot. He screams, the noise filling the Hole, echoing around us. Finn whips around, his eyes wide and furious as he slams the butt of his pistol against Dustin's temple.

I gape at him, and all the anger in me bubbles up. His gaze swings to me, unrepentant. "Take care of him, while he can't bring every infect in miles to us."

He throws me a first aid kit, and I catch it, even in my daze. Collin crouches next to me and helps me wrestle Dustin's boot off his swollen foot. I prod it, but the truth is I don't know what the hell I'm doing.

"Just wrap it tight," Collin says, and I latch on to his instructions. As I wind the bandage around Dustin's foot, Collin shoves a pillow under his head—I guess neither of the boys wants to move him. Can't blame them much. Dustin is solid.

"What the fuck are we doing?" I demand in a harsh whisper. He gives me a curious look, and I glance over at Finn. "He's not stable, Collin. He's *violent.*"

"He saved our lives," Collin answers.

"Why didn't you tell me about this?"

"You didn't need to know, and Finn asked me not to." Collin's voice is reasonable and calm, and I want to scream and shake him. I'm anything *but* reasonable and calm.

"Ren, I know how you feel about Finn. I get it— you hate him. But can you just put that aside for a few days? We're not in normal circumstances, and you sniping at him every few minutes isn't going to help any of us." Collin says.

I stare at him, seeing the exhaustion and fear in his eyes I hadn't noticed before. I reach for him, squeeze his hand. "Go sleep," I tell him, and he shakes his head.

"She's right. You haven't had more than thirty minutes in almost two days. Go. I'll take first watch," Finn says from behind me, and I force myself not to react, schooling my expression to impassivity. Collin looks between us, uncertain, and then he nods.

The silence that fills the Hole after Collin collapses is almost deafening. Finn moves around, comfortable in his own space, unpacking bags and setting out weapons. I feel, suddenly, the itchy sensation of dried sweat, and I'm anxious to get out of my restrictive clothing.

"Is there somewhere I can change?" I ask, and Finn pauses, looking at me, one eyebrow arched in question. Something flickers in his gaze, shut down too quickly for me to follow.

"The back—past the kitchen is a tunnel. Change there. Should be some water to rinse, if you want."

I start to say thanks, but he's already turned away. Asshat.

I strip quickly, in almost complete darkness, and shiver—it's cool back here, surprisingly so. I dip my hands into the chilly water and scrub the dust of the day from my skin. It's not enough to get rid of the dirty feeling, but it helps a little. I shiver and dress quickly in a long pair of sweats and a loose shirt, leaving my bra and zom gear in a pile on the stone. Then I pad back out into the main area of the cave and scoop up my knives and guns. The latter go on the table with Finn and Collin's for cleaning, and then I go to stand near Finn. He's at the entrance of the cave, staring into the night.

"Thanks," I say, abruptly, and his gaze darts to me. "For getting Collin out."

He gives me a thin-lipped smile. "Not for yourself?"

I look away, into the night, and ask the question that's been at the back of my mind all day. "What were you doing in the orchards?"

Finn is so quiet and still, I look over and check on him—seeing him startles me.

"Collin and I have always had a plan, in case of a major breach. Getting you was part of the plan."

I nod and look back into the darkness. "What happens next?"

"You go to bed."

His voice is different, subtly shut off, and I push myself to my feet. I don't particularly want to be sitting here having a conversation with Finn O'Malley anyway.

As I turn away, his voice stops me. "What you did back there—Nurrin, that was stupid."

"You could say thank you."

He moves, catching my bare ankle in a vice-like grip. "I won't thank you for putting yourself in danger." Finn's voice is low, a soft accent rounding his words. His thumb moves over my ankle, and my pulse jumps—I wonder if he's even aware of the caress and what game he's playing if he is.

"Why do you call me that?" I demand, instead. His finger stills, and he releases me, rising in one smooth, almost inhuman move. He crowds me, and I step back until I bump into the side of the cave wall. His presence is choking the air in my lungs, consuming everything around me, and I want to shove him away, but the look in his dark eyes stops me—there's something there I've never seen before. Something I don't want to think about. I tilt my chin up, glaring, and Finn smiles, a faint twitch of his lips.

And steps away from me. "Ren is the name of a little girl avoiding who she is. What she was born to. Nurrin—that's the name of a woman who risks her life because she's got more courage than sense and was born to epic times and deeds."

I gape at him as he turns away, and I know he's aware of me staring, questions burning on the tip of my tongue. But he doesn't turn back to me, and his voice is remote and disdainful as he says, "Get some sleep, Nurrin. Tomorrow is going to be a long day."

I retreat to the couch, cuddling into Dustin and pulling a blanket up over us. He curls around me, an arm snaking over my waist, and I smile, kissing his hair.

When I look up, I'm stunned to find Finn staring at us, his eyes furious and hot. Before I can say anything—before I can draw breath—he turns away, watching for dangers in the night.

Chapter 11

Conversations and Threats

I'm awakened by voices and heat. Dustin has kicked the blanket off sometime in the night, but the heat rolling off him is more than enough to make me sweat. I ease away from him enough to give me breathing room.

"We can wait it out, Collin. It's safer here than anywhere, you know that."

There's a long moment of silence, and then, "Do you really think Ren'll go for that?" Collin's voice is quiet, and Finn doesn't answer. I peek up over the couch and see them—Finn sitting at the small table, his back to me as they clean the guns. Light is streaming into the cave, and I can smell coffee.

"She'll do what she's told. But it'll go down easier if you're the one telling," Finn says lazily, and all my anger sparks again. "Also, she's listening to us."

Heat floods my cheeks as I stand, dusting off my gritty palms. Collin raises, coming to give me a quick hug. "Do you want some coffee?"

"I'd like to know what I'm being told to do. What am I supposed to listen to.?" I snap, aiming the words at Finn's head.

Collin has the grace to flush, but all Finn says is, "Eavesdropping is a bad habit—and the sign of a morally corrupt character."

"You'd do it in a heartbeat."

He finally glances at me, and for some reason, all I can see is the expression in his eyes when he watched me on the couch last night. "It's said imitation is the sincerest form of flattery," he says silkily.

"Imitate this," I snap and flip him off. A smile twitches his lips before he turns back to the weapons on the table in front of him. That quickly, I'm dismissed.

I follow my nose to the coffee on the counter, pouring a cup and pulling myself onto the solid rock ledge before sipping it. Thick, hot, black as night—just the way I love it. "So, what were you talking about?"

Finn and Collin exchange one of those wordless glances that bugs the shit out of me, and I look away.

And scream.

The boys bolt into action, guns immediately leveled at the cave entry, Collin planted in front of me, scanning for an infect. I slide down, pushing past him, and stumble-run to the entrance of the cave. Finn catches me as I lean over the lip—and I'm glad. The site makes me nauseated. He pulls me away, but not before I see the gorge yawing below us, the sides of the canyon stained with blood and infection, the broken bits of infects who have fallen over the cliff.

"What was that?" he hisses, shaking me.

"*Finn,*" Collin snaps, and Finn releases me abruptly. I sag against the wall, struggling not to throw up.

"She doesn't know, man. She has no idea what the hell is going on—you need to lighten up," Collin says, his voice tight and angry. I've never heard him this angry with Finn before, and it cheers me up a little. Until he turns on me. "And you need to get your shit together, Ren. That stunt yesterday? Forget what Finn'll do to you, you try that again, I'll kick your ass myself. Screams like that in the Wide Open will get us killed."

"There was infect out there," I protest, and he rolls his eyes.

"We're here for a reason, Ren. They can't *get us here.*"

Suddenly, the previous day, the stress of everything slams into me. Collin yelling at me never fails to make me emotional. I turn away, compressing my lips and blinking furiously. I won't let him see me cry. Him or Finn fucking O'Malley. I hunch my shoulders when he reaches for me, pulling out of his reach. Silence fills the cave, making it seem smaller than it truly is, and I want to bolt—want to run the three mile track in Hellspawn, anything that will let me work out some of this emotion.

Even punching Finn a few times would help, but I think he hits back.

That settles the last of my emotions, and I finally turn around and face Collin. I continue to ignore Finn—it's probably the best option available to me.

"Dustin's got an infection," I say.

Chapter 12

Infection

They wake him up.

Despite my protest that it's probably just dirt in the gash on his arm, Finn shakes him awake. Dustin blinks blearily, a sleepy smile on his lips. Finn says, his voice flatly unemotional, "You have a live infection. Strip down for examination and possible quarantine."

"Quarantine?" I demand, amused. "Where are you going to stick him? He was with Collin in that car for almost twelve hours. If he's going into Q, Collin would too."

I don't say that I slept next Dustin, or that putting them into Q would leave Finn and me alone together and we'd end up killing each other, and wouldn't the infects just love that. I think he gets it, though, because his lips do that twitchy thing again that makes me think he's going to smile, but he doesn't.

Heaven forbid Finn O'Malley show a human emotion other than anger.

"I wasn't bit," Dustin groans, putting a hand up to block the sun streaming into his eyes. I take an involuntary step forward, and Collin catches me. He's not taking any chances, not until they've satisfied their suspicions.

Dustin looks at me, and I bite my lip. "Just do it, Dustin. Please?"

He pushes himself upright, and I see the large bruise on his temple from where Finn hit him last night. Finn approaches him and takes a quick blood sample to run against markers of ERI-Milan infection.

It was an experiment the army played with at first—that eventually spilled into the private sector. Sanelos Pharmaceuticals created an emotion inhibitor to keep soldiers even keeled on the battlefield and during deployment. But

Sanelos saw a civilian market. Kids were too emotional, too high strung. Prone to random acts of violence and suicide. The emotional response inhibitor was the magic pill—pop one and settle your ass down. Soccer moms around the country swore by it; the government used it to calm the violent and criminally insane; the military gave it to the soldiers with a touch of PTSD—it was the wonder drug that gave people back their lives, albeit without much in the way of emotion.

Because it wasn't just violence—the ERI pill killed all emotion. And kill wasn't the right word— it muted them, diverted the chemical reaction to keep the subject calm. It was the perfect solution, until it wasn't.

The first case of ERI mutation was in Emilie Milan, a little fourteen-year-old ballet dancer. She'd been on ERI for ten years—one of the first poster children for the drug—when she was killed in a car accident on the way to a ballet recital. When she woke up, high on adrenaline, and attacked the morgue attendant, it was the first sign ERI wasn't the savior everyone thought it was.

That was the day I was born. Something about the long use of ERI mutated in Emilie, and it spread when she bit the morgue worker. ERI-Milan spread like wildfire, the infection working through the dead and bringing them back with a violent hunger.

Within days, thousands were dead—and coming back. Hoards of infects were racing through towns and cities. And on Third Day, as it collided with the military—one of the largest users of ERI—it changed the response in the soldiers. There was something about the pack of people that changed the virus, mutating it. If ERI-Milan was the beginning, the horde colliding with the army outside of Atlanta—that was the end.

"He's not bitten," Finn announces, and I twitch, jerked from my thoughts. "Get dressed, Dustin."

"I told you that," I can't help but snipe, and Collin gives me a quiet, quelling stare. I shrug. I wait, my back turned as Dustin struggles to redress. Finally, I hear the soft rasp of his jeans, and I turn back to him, going to sit next to him on the couch. His arm comes around me, and I snuggle into his side, ignoring the surprise in Collin's eyes. "So he's not infected with ERI-Milan. He still has a blood infection."

Finn walks out of the back tunnel carrying a syringe. His eyes find me, and his expression tightens then goes savagely blank. The vial of blood is gone, but he carries a test strip. I snatch it from him as he injects Dustin, checking it quickly. None of the markers are there—absolutely no sign of ERI-Milan. A sigh of relief slips from me, and Dustin squeezes me closer.

"This will help—but I can't promise it'll fix everything," Finn says.

"Then why don't we take him to Haven 7? It's not far. They'll have a doctor for Dustin, and it's safe there."

Collin and Finn exchange a glance, and I feel my brother nod. Finn's gaze swings to me. "Why do you presume that Haven 7 will be safe?"

"Havens are built to be safe."

"Hellspawn wasn't, yesterday."

The quietly spoken words hit me like a hammer, and I inhale sharply. Dustin glares. "Dude. Chill. She's going on the same assumption we've had most of our lives."

"She needs to change her assumptions," Finn says ruthlessly. "The Havens are falling, Nurrin. Hellspawn was just the latest in a list of nine to fall this year."

I'm glad I'm sitting—I'd fall if I weren't. As it is, I feel like the cave is spinning, and bile churns in my gut. Finn is watching me, and Dustin is cursing at my side. Collin looks so sad and tired. Why is Finn still watching me—like my reaction matters right now? I close my eyes and force out the question, "Nine—how many dead?"

"There were a handful of survivors from three of the Havens. Twenty total."

I jerk away from Dustin, stumbling to the back of the cave. It's not solitude, but it's as close as I can get. I fall to my knees, the numbers spinning through my head.

After the initial wave, when the infection spread like wildfire, the governments swept in, putting people behind fences. With only a fraction of the population still left alive—less than one percent of the population survived the first six months—they divided us into segments and set up Havens. For nine to fall in six months—the sheer number of lives lost makes me sick, and I gag, throwing up.

A hand is on my back, and I push against Collin, tears burning in my eyes. "How long has this been going on?"

He doesn't answer for a long time. "About a year. The first few reports, we thought were flukes. Aggressive infects."

"And now?"

He shrugs. "Finn explains it better. Come back out." I stare at him, and he gives an aggravated sigh. "He's not as awful as you want to think. And he got us out of Hellspawn before it fell."

"What's his end game?" I ask, quietly. If it were anyone but Finn, I'd say Collin was—the devotion he shows my brother has actually made me consider the possibility that Finn bats for the same team I do. But he's never made a secret of his open bedroom door and the women who parade in and out of it.

Collin looks away. "You'd have to ask Finn that."

He stands, and I follow him out of the tunnel, back into the main cave.

Chapter 13

Map of the World

Dustin is exhausted, so I help him into the bed that Collin slept in last night. "How do you feel?" I ask, hovering anxiously over him.

"Tired," he slurs. He forces his eyes to focus, and a vague smile turns his lips. "Biters, Ren, you're so gorgeous."

I flush, and he laughs, tugging at me. I kiss him, briefly, before I shove him down, and he laughs, sleepily, before he settles and closes his eyes. I roll mine and stomp back to the kitchen table, snatching up my snub nose revolver. Finn is unfolding a map, and I lean over it. It's the United States, pre-Infection. But dotted across the continent are Havens, and I shiver, my fingers brushing the bright yellow stickers that are faded and curling with age. I press one down, rubbing my thumb over the eight scrawled on the little dot. Finn nudges me a little, and I step away, to Collin's side. Finn ignores my retreat, leaning over the map and drawing a brilliant red x over Haven 8.

I let my gaze sweep over the map, finding the other eight Havens that have fallen. They form a line, starting just south of us, and marching north. Hellspawn is the farthest they've gotten. My gaze shoots up, collides with Finn's. His lips are compressed, and what I see in his dark eyes makes my stomach bottom out.

"They're cutting the west off," I say.

He nods, and the confirmation makes it worse somehow. I fall into a seat and stare at the map, hoping that it will change. It doesn't.

"We have to tell the north," I murmur, absently.

"No."

My head snaps up, and I stare at Finn. He's shaking his head, implacable, and a hysterical laugh burns in the back of my throat. "Why the hell not?" I demand.

"They don't want to hear it, Ren," Collin says, and I twist to look at him. "They won't accept it. And if we show up at Haven 12, telling them we're survivors from Haven 8, they'll throw us in Q. We don't have time for that."

"Excuse me, but we're sitting in a cave in the middle of the desert. How different is this from sitting in Q?"

"We decide when we leave," Finn answers. I snort.

"*You* decide, you mean."

He nods, and I rub my eyes, too exhausted to even be angry. "So what do you want to do?"

"I have contacts, in the west. I want to use them—we can still evacuate the west and move the Havens south. Let the biters have it."

"They'll follow us," I protest.

"When in the past twenty years hasn't that been true?"

"So what do you want to do?"

"I want to go to Haven 18. I can talk to some folks I know there—if we *can* evacuate the west, our best bet is to start there."

"Then let's go," I say, standing. "The sooner we get Dustin some medical help, the better."

Finn is silent, and Collin shifts, looking at him. "It's as safe as it's going to get, O'Malley."

"I'm going alone."

Chapter 14

Threat Assessment

I sit with my legs dangling out of the cave.

The sun is setting, and the cool air is seeping into me, chilling the stone under my ass. Collin is preparing canned soup for dinner, ignoring Finn.

"Get away from the ledge," Finn orders irritably when he walks out of the back tunnel. I'm proud of myself for not flipping him off, although I'm not sure Collin is still sticking with the "be nice" routine.

When I don't move, Finn hooks his hands under my armpits and drags me away. I shriek, flailing in his grip. He scoops me off the ground and tosses me onto the couch. I bounce up, swinging, and he ducks away, a savage grin toying with the edges of his lips.

"Want to fight, little girl?" he taunts, and I swing again. He back away, and I spin, kicking him with all the force I can put behind it. Finn grunts as my foot collides with his gut, and I drop into a crouch, my hair spilling into my eyes. His are furious—and something else. "Don't fucking touch me, you bastard," I snarl, and he has the gall to laugh at me.

Collin jerks him away from me. "*Finn,*" he snaps, and I see what makes my brother a Walker, the barely leashed violence that's threatening to explode. "Cool it, man. You're pushing me too far."

Finn's gaze focuses on him, slowly, then flickers to me and back again. He nods, and I turn away. Collin catches me, concern written on his face. I shrug him off. My nerves are shot, and I wish he'd let the fight happen.

Sure, Finn could wipe the floor with my ass, but at least I'd be able to get some of this aggression out. I desperately need that.

Even killing zombies would help right now.

We scatter with our soup, and I carry mine into the bedroom. Dustin's sweating. I check his bandage—it's tight, cutting into his skin. I swallow hard as I put my dinner aside, and then I unwrap the bandage.

The stench makes me gag, and I almost lose the little I've eaten. The flesh is putrid, decaying, his skin stretched and inflamed around the scratch. A line of thick pus oozes out, and I use a clean corner of his bandage to wipe it away.

"His cut—it had to come from one of the infects."

I glance over at Finn. He stands in the doorway, staring at me. I don't address his words— if it's true, and it really is the only reason Dustin would have this kind of infection this quickly, there's still a chance he'll turn.

Unless he's given meds, and quickly.

I clean his wound, dumping almost an entire bottle of alcohol on it. When Dustin begins to thrash, Finn pushes away from the wall and comes to hold him still. I glance at him quickly, and then away, wiping and pouring, until the bottle is empty. Finn cleans up the rags and trash as I re-wrap Dustin's arm, and then he grabs my cold soup. I follow him out of the room.

And begin to plan my argument.

Chapter 15

Making My Case

I wait until Collin is asleep before I get up from the couch and make my way to where Finn is sitting with his back propped against the cave wall, taking first watch.

Even if he claims we're safe, in the Wide Open, there is always a watch.

"You need sleep," he says without looking at me.

"So do you. You had watch last night."

He finally graces me with a look, and I meet it with a cool one of my own.

"What do you want, Nurrin?"

"You're going to Haven 18, to launch the evacuation." He doesn't respond, and his gaze goes back into the night. But the stillness of him tells me he's listening. Finn O'Malley is always listening.

"Here's the thing—you go, you leave Collin with an open infection. Dustin needs meds, you know that. And you won't be back in time—the infection is going to spread, and eventually, he's going to turn."

"He's still not showing the markers."

"A flesh wound is still exposure. It takes longer, and we can stop it, but if we don't do anything, it's going to happen. And you won't be back before then."

His gaze swings to me. "What do you want, Nurrin?"

"Take me with you," I say softly, and his nostrils flare, his expression tight. "Or Collin. I know you—you wouldn't be headed to Haven 18 if you didn't have a way out. Take Collin and let him bring back the meds." I hesitate, and then, "*Please,* Finn."

"That means leaving you with a live infection," he says emotionlessly.

I shrug. "Dustin won't hurt me. And the infection won't take hold for at least a week. Collin will be back in plenty of time."

He stares at me, his eyes unfathomable, and then he shakes his head, and the tension eases out of him. "Go to bed, Nurrin. We'll talk about this in the morning."

I want to protest, but something in his gaze when I open my mouth is dangerous and forbidding. So I swallow my argument and stand up to walk away.

Before I do, I say softly, "I'll get the meds Dustin needs. If you won't take me or Collin, I'll go by myself. You won't be here to stop me. Think about that before you vanish into the Wide Open by yourself."

Chapter 16

Executive Decision

Collin shakes me awake, and for a moment, half-asleep and surrounded by my brother's voice and the scent of coffee, I can pretend I'm still in the Hive, still safe behind the walls of Hellspawn. Then Finn curses and the distinct sound of a gun being loaded fills the cave, and the illusion vanishes. I sit up and rub my eyes.

Finn spares me a glance, and I cross my arms over my thin tank top, wishing I'd had time to grab something more substantial. "Get dressed, Nurrin. We're leaving for Haven 18 in ten minutes."

I blink at him, and then, "But you're taking Collin."

Finn gives me a dark smile, and I flinch away from him. "There is no way in hell I'm leaving you alone in this cave with a live infection, Nurrin. You'd either bring a horde down the canyon, or Dustin would kill you. Neither would please me. So get your pretty ass off my couch and dressed. *Now.*"

I flush, and I hate myself for it—that was his intention. To Finn O'Malley, everything is a weapon, even words and emotions. It's one of the things I admire about him, even if I do despise it.

"I don't *want* to go," I say, shrilly.

Finn laughs at that, a deep belly laugh that makes me flinch—it's coated in irony and danger. The idea of spending hours in a car with him, days at Haven 18, of being *dependent* on this man—I shudder and look at Collin, my eyes pleading. He looks away.

Disbelief slips through me. "You want me to go with him?"

Collin shrugs. "Staying here with an open infection isn't much safer. He'll protect you."

"I'll kill him," I snarl.

Finn pushes against me from the rear, and I skid forward, away from him, but he catches me by the waist, hauling me against him, and whispers his threat directly into my ear. "You can try."

His breath tickles the shell of my ear, stirs my hair, and goose bumps break out over my skin. I yank myself out of his grip and retreat to the curtained-off bedroom. I can hear Collin and Finn talking.

What the hell was that?

For a moment, under his constant aggression, there had been something playful—almost—in Finn. And that was terrifying.

"Five minutes, Nurrin!" He yells, and I shake myself. A quick glance at Dustin confirms nothing has changed—his fever is high, and the bandage on his arm is bloody and reeks of rot.

I don't really have a choice. If I don't go, Dustin'll die. I'd endure anything to avoid that.

I strip quickly, wiggling into a pair of tight cargo pants, a simple black bra, and a tank top. I pull on one of Collin's old button down shirts, leaving it unbuttoned, then grab my boots.

In the main room, the boys are talking—Finn is giving orders, and Collin is nodding, shoving food and weapons into a bag. Finally he snaps, "I know, Finn. I've done this before. Worry about yourself and my sister."

Finn's voice lowers a little, and I pause in the act of tying my boot. I wonder if his expression softens to match. "I won't let anything happen to her, Collin. You know that."

He does? How? The friendship that I never liked, never understood, makes even less sense now that I'm spending time with them together.

"I know you'll do everything you can to keep her safe," Collin says, "but this is Ren we're talking about. She's not going to listen to you—she isn't like the other Hive girls."

"I know," Finn says, his voice full of something I don't bother to assess.

I slide my other boot on and tie it quickly, then kiss Dustin's clammy forehead. "Hang on, babe. I'll be back." Without letting myself consider if that's true or not, I exit the room.

Finn is waiting, giving me a quick look before nodding his approval. I grab the bag Collin holds out and force myself to meet his gaze.

His eyes are tight, worried, and it makes my stomach churn. He pulls me into a fierce hug, and I bury my nose in his chest, memorizing the feel of him, the smell of sweat and gun powder that surrounds my brother. "Listen to him," he murmurs in my ear, and I make a noise of protest. His grip tightens. "I mean it, Ren. He can keep you safe, but you have to trust him. You won't have anyone else out there, and I need you to survive and come back to me."

"Let's go," Finn says abruptly, and Collin releases me. I stumble and Finn catches me, reflexively.

"You have your weapons?" Collin says and, for a heartbeat, I'm back in the Hive, leaving for another day in the orchards while he passes out after walking the wall. I blink back tears and reach for my snub-nosed revolver. The knife goes into my boot, several throwing stars get tucked into my butt pocket, and I loop a shotgun over my head, to hang on my back.

Collin nods, and it's time.

Chapter 17

Topside

The wind is whistling, and it's throwing my perception off. Finn edges up the thin path, peering over the rim of the canyon. His tense shoulders ease a fraction, and he murmurs, softly, "It's clear. Move fast—don't stop, not for anything. Get in the car and turn it on."

"But," I begin.

"No," he snaps, "you don't get to argue. Let's get this straight right now: out here, you listen. You don't question what I say, you do it. If you can't handle that, go back to the Hole and get ready to kill your best friend."

I clench my teeth and nod shortly. Finn gives me a feral smile then peers over the edge again.

He explodes onto the surface, already shooting. I'm a half step behind him, running through the infects as Finn puts them down. The Porsche is gleaming, if a little dented. I slide into the front seat, slamming the door shut behind me and fumbling with the key. It slides in despite my shaking fingers, and I scream as something collides with the driver side of the car. An infect slides down the door as Finn shoves a knife into the base of its skull. He opens the door, and I hurl one of my throwing stars without thinking, nicking his arm before it lands in the eye of the infect behind him. He doesn't bother looking—he slips into the car and slams his foot onto the gas before he's even got the door shut.

"You tore my shirt," Finn says. I've finally got my heart rate under control, but his voice kicks it back up.

"But I did kill the infect," I say in my defense, and his lips twitch.

"You did what you were told—I didn't expect that."

"I said I would," I say defensively, flushing when he rolls his eyes. "I *do* take orders, when they make sense."

"Like when Hellspawn was breached?"

That still bothers me. He shouldn't have been in the Orchard—even if they had a protocol in place, a plan to get us out. "How did you get there so quickly?" I blurt out, and his eyes snap to mine.

They're gray—a sharp, cold gray, like the sky over the wall at first light.

The thought is absurd, and I don't know why I'm noticing, why now of all times. I flush and look out the window. "Your house wasn't close to the Orchards."

"Who said I was home?" he answers, looking back out the windshield.

Irritation sparks through me, and I look away as he laughs, sharp and mocking. "There are some benefits to the privacy of the orchards—benefits you don't find in the Hive."

A girl. He was in the Orchard with a *girl?*

Heat floods my cheeks, and I twist away from him, furious and hating that I am.

"How long, to get to Haven 18?"

His lips do that irritating twitch again. "Two days, Nurrin. Get comfortable."

That makes me nervous. Two *days*, trapped in this tiny car with Finn's overly large presence? I look out the window as he slams the car forward. Infects are swarming toward us, and time seems to slow as the car speeds up. One catches my eyes as he races at us, his skin limp and hanging off his limbs in long, leathery strips. His left leg is twisted horribly, and I can see bone, but it doesn't slow him as he throws himself against the Porsche. The car skids a little at the impact, and I see the terrible hunger and rage in the zombie's eyes as Finn curses savagely, wrestling the car into submission and jerking forward. There's a sick snap when we roll over something in the road, and I glance at him, worried, but his eyes are tight on the road—if it can even be called that—as we leave the zombies—and my brother—behind.

We travel in silence. I keep my gun in my lap, but, though we see small herds of zombies occasionally, they don't give chase often, and when they do, the Porsche easily out paces them. Even a zombie will give up, after a while.

Eventually, I relax, stop scanning the desert for infects, and survey the interior of the car. The seat I'm sitting in is soft, buttery leather cocooning me. The interior is midnight black, and it makes Finn's pale skin and startling eyes stand out in the dimness. He glances at me, as if feeling my gaze, and I flush, looking away.

And somehow, it changes the mood in the car. He doesn't say a word, but there's a tension now that wasn't here minutes ago. I shift in my seat then curse myself for doing that. There's a radio on his dash, though it's useless. Radio died with the rest of the world, when I was born.

"I'm hungry," I say, and Finn's lips twitch again.

"There's some energy bars in my bag," is all he says, and I twist, my ass in the air as I shuffle through the bags we threw into the miniscule back when we jumped into the car. I let out a soft cry of triumph and slide down into my seat, sitting sideways, facing him with two energy bars.

"I've got peanut butter and chocolate, and tropical fruit," I say, reading them. "You can pick, as long as you don't want chocolate."

I grin at him—and freeze. His expression, which has been neutral for most of the morning, is cold, icy and remote, and I shiver involuntarily. It draws his gaze, which flicks over me with a touch of heat that defies the coldness in him.

"Finn?" I ask, my voice cautious.

His gaze goes back to the road, and his voice is deliberately easy. "Chocolate. I don't eat tropical fruit shit."

I hesitate, and he holds out a hand, like he can snap his fingers and I'll immediately cave.

That they *are* his energy bars doesn't really matter much. I open the chocolate bar, and the smell slams into me. My stomach rumbles alarmingly, and Finn laughs, a sound that tickles my belly and sends butterflies to flight.

I break the bar and hand the smaller portion to him. Finn's eyes narrow, and he gives me a disbelieving stare. I shrug. "I'm a girl."

He opens his mouth to answer when it happens. The pop is loud—deafening in the silence of the desert—and the Porsche spins, skidding under the blown tire. My seat belt snaps me back as Finn curses, fighting for control of the car. Dust explodes around us as we skid off the road, into the soft dirt of the desert, and I close my eyes as we come to a stop.

"*Fuck!*" Finn snarls and explodes from the car. He's moving fast, and I struggle to keep up.

"Do we have a spare?" I demand, and he grunts, already half under the Porsche. I couldn't imagine him out in the Wide Open without something as basic as a spare tire.

A screech jerks my attention away from him as the tire slides out from under the car. I whip around and see them—four infects. Two large men, a girl who could have been my age when she turned, a little boy no older than eight. They move with an eerie beauty and grace, and aside from that initial scream, they are silent as they race toward us. I pull my snub-nosed revolver, line my sights and fire.

The little boy falls, and the girl freezes, staring at his prone body. Something twists in her expression when she looks back up, a snarl on her lips. Finn emerges from the car, breathless, and I snatch his crossbow as he throws it up at me. "Hurry," I urge and bring the weapon up, firing twice in rapid succession. The male in the lead squeals when the first bolt lodges in his shoulder, and then the second embeds in his eye, spinning him around and killing his cry as he goes down like a sack of bricks. His pack mates hesitate, hissing, and I take a deep breath, aiming.

The scream the girl let out is so loud, and so unexpected, I jolt, firing inadvertently. It slams into her chest, and her scream gurgles off in a furious whine. Her eyes are full of hatred when she meets my gaze, a hungry, unthinking hatred that hits me like a hammer.

"Focus, Ren," Finn orders from near my hip, and it jerks me from my paralysis. Putting the other two down is easy after that, though the female lands disturbingly close to Finn's boot-clad feet. I step over, straddling his legs as I watch the puffs of dust on the desert. There are a lot—more than I think I can handle, and they're getting closer.

Drawn by the infect's angry scream.

"Hurry, O'Malley," I snap, and he grunts. Then the zombies are here—close enough I can put them down. I keep count for the first eight. After that, there are too many, too close, and as fast as I fire, there are more. The world seems to slow when I empty my clip. I drop the gun next to Finn's boots and pull my knives as the zombies swarm me. I shove the blade into the first's eye and grab him, pulling his limp corpse close to shield me as I attack the others. For a few minutes, straddling

Finn, embracing a corpse and killing the infects, I think I can do this. Then one lunges at me from atop the Porsche and I scream as I duck away from her teeth. Her long fingers catch in my shoulder, and I feel the skin tear, feel the burn of the wound. Rage crystallizes into icy precision, and I hurl the zombie away from me and slam my blade into the infect that jumped me. "O'Malley, we gotta go!" I yell, reaching for and hurling my throwing stars. I'm running dangerously low on weapons, and I can't fall back—they are already trying to slide past me, attack Finn where he is defenseless on the ground. Retreating would be a death sentence.

"Two minutes," he yells, and I kick the face of a infect who fell near him, scrabbling for a booted foot.

"*Now!*""

"Get in the car," he orders a heartbeat—a lifetime—later, and I laugh outright. No way in hell.

"Damn it, Ren, you promised!" he snarls, rolling to his knees and pulling his gun. The noise will draw more infects, but at this point, it might kill enough for us to get away, and that matters more than silence.

"When I said that, we weren't under attack."

He mutters something, and there's a brief lull in his firing before I hear the door swing open. An infect rushes me, and I swallow a shriek of pain as the exposed bones of his fingers break the skin, my blood spraying in a rush.

The remaining infects screech, and I slam my knife into the zombie's eye. A warm arm wraps around my waist, and I do scream as Finn pulls me into his lap and slams the door behind us.

I don't even have time to scramble out of his lap before he floors the gas and we explode from the horde in a burst of decaying bodies and dust.

Chapter 18

Somewhere Safe

My hands are shaking, adrenaline coursing through my body, and a random, awful thought hits me: *is this what it's like for the infects?*

A laugh burns in my throat, and I swallow hard, trying not to let it out, trying not to throw up. My arm and back are itchy, burning, and I jerk around so violently it jars Finn.

I'm still in his lap. How the fuck did I forget that I was in his lap? His arms are around me, holding the steering wheel. His face is close—close enough that I can see the tiny freckles I never knew he had, the muscles tightening in his jaw, the stubble, dark like his hair, on his jaw. His gray eyes flick up to mine, hot and hungry and furious.

Startled, I almost fall off his lap and into my seat. He shifts a little. "You weren't bitten."

It's a statement, and I'm not sure if he's denying it as a possibility or stating something he's observed. Either way, I shake my head. I wasn't. "But I was scratched."

He holds out his hand, and I give him my arm without saying anything in complaint. He examines the claw marks, the deep grooves that are still leaking blood, and I flush, trying to pull away—it's revolting. Finn's grip tightens, almost painfully, and he looks at me, furious.

"I told you to get in the car."

"You could have died," I answered, without thinking. "Those zombies were trying to get to your feet, your legs. You couldn't have gotten clear of them."

He doesn't say anything for a long moment, and I twist, digging in the bags to find the first aid kit. I drop down into my seat with it and rip open a handful of alcohol wipes. They aren't the best thing to use—acid would be, I think—but they'll do for the moment. The wipes burn, and I hiss, my eyes watering. He's still staring out the windshield, his jaw tight, and I sigh, wrapping a bandage around my arm. The bleeding has begun to slow, and I think it'll be enough to tide me over until we get to Haven 18.

Maybe.

"You could say thank you," I say, reaching around to swipe at my shoulder blade ineffectually.

Finn stares at me for a solid thirty seconds, and I realize what an idiot I must look like, before he finally shakes his head and looks away. "I told you, Nurrin. I won't thank you for risking your life. Follow your damn orders before you get us both killed."

He gentles the words, a little, by taking a clean wipe and rubbing my wounds. I gasp at the ruthless cleaning, but then he drops the wipe, and his fingers ghost over the cut before he pulls his hand back abruptly.

"You'll have a scar. Two of them."

I shrug and look away. "I'd have a lot more, if I walked the wall."

A grin tugs at his lip, and I shiver under the gray gaze he sends my way. "You want to be a Wall Walker?"

"Why not?"

"Collin would never let you." He laughs, like I'm an amusing joke. Or his best friend's little sister, playing with the big boy's toys. Heat flares through me, and something makes me shift in my seat, leaning over until my lips hovered a few inches from his ear. He is still—so still it seems obscene that we are moving.

"I didn't need Collin to sponsor me. And I didn't need you, O'Malley. I would have walked on my own."

His gaze is dark, his lips so close to mine I can feel the air move when he demands, "Who the fuck was sponsoring you?"

I drop back into my seat and shrug, a little. "I would have found someone."

He gives me a disbelieving stare, and I lean my seat back a few inches—as far as it'll allow me to. "Wake me up when we get...there." I wave a hand vaguely at the desert sprawling before us, and then I curl over on my side, tugging Collin's shirt around me as I fall asleep.

The car slowing wakes me, and I jerk upright in the seat, my hand reaching automatically for my weapon. My heart stops when I remember, and I can't help the hiss of air.

"What?"

He doesn't bother to ask if I've slept well, and I sort of resent that. He's above mundane trivialities that seem to dominate the lives of everyone else.

I answer anyway, "My gun. I left it there, when we were attacked."

He doesn't even look away from the road. "You can get a new one at Haven 18. Or use one of mine—I have plenty."

I don't tell him that isn't the point—that this gun is special because Collin gave it to me, that it was the first thing he gave me after our mother turned. That it was hers. That it told me, more than words ever could, I was safe and loved and not alone in this fucked up world.

I shove those thoughts aside and look around. We're approaching a field of windmills, and I wonder if that's where we will rest for the night.

That we will stop is beyond dispute. I can see exhaustion pulling at Finn like an anxious lover and feel the shadows shifting with bodies ripe with death and disease.

"Where are we going?" I ask, more to ease the boredom than from any real desire to know.

Finn glances at me briefly. "Somewhere safe."

I want to pry, to ask for more than that, but I'm too tired, and I ache. It's a deep, uneasy feeling in my shoulder and in my arm, and I want to scratch at them.

I wonder if Finn would notice, if I did. His eyes are firmly on the road, but that means very little when we're talking about Finn.

He drives through the windmill fields, past the great turbines that power the western Havens, and turns into a forest.

It makes my breath catch, and it hits me suddenly that we aren't in the desert anymore. The trees press up against the car doors, making me anxious for my gun.

"It's safe," Finn says, and I look at him. He shrugs. "At least, as safe as anything can be."

The lake startles me. It gleams in the moonlight—night is settling on the forest, the last light slipping from the sky and giving way to darkness. I stare at the water and wonder what the hell he plans to do. We skirt the lake for a mile or more, and I laugh when I see the houseboat. It's small, but it'll take us into the water, and that's really all we need.

Infects avoid water.

Finn eases the car up to the dock and reaches behind us, pulling our bags from the depths of the car and into our laps. I peer into the darkness, but aside from the trees and tall grass, its quiet, an eerie peacefulness that makes my stomach churn. What's out there, in the darkness?

"You ready?" he asks, and I shift, adjusting my bag and reaching for my gun. He stops me, handing me a long machete instead. "Keep it quiet."

I nod, and we slip out of the car and into the surprisingly cool night. Faster than I could believe possible, Finn is at my side, herding me toward the boat. The dock is short—a dozen yards—but leaves me feeling itchy and exposed. I breathe a sigh of relief when I step onto the houseboat, feeling its slight shift under me. Finn tosses me his bag, and I swallow down a scream of pain as it yanks at my torn arm.

The boat is quiet—it barely makes a noise as we pull away from the dock and idle out to the exposed open water of the lake. I feel the shore receding—and some of my worries with it. Here, at least, we're safe for a few hours. Here we can both sleep and not set a watch. Here, there are no threats.

Finn is finally satisfied with our location in the lake and kills the motor. We bob slightly as he throws an anchor out, and then silence settles over the lake and forest again.

Finn stares out over the water for a long moment. I wonder what he is thinking, but when I shift, he looks up.

"Let's get below and get your wounds stitched up."

I freeze, staring at him. "You aren't stitching me."

Finn gives me a dark smile, and I shiver from the menace in it. I clutch my bag tighter and head for the stairs. Six short steps down empties me into a small room—small enough that there is little room to move around the bed that dominates the space.

"Sit down," he says, and without thinking, I obey, dropping onto the bed in exhaustion. He rifles around the miniscule bathroom and brings out a first aid kit.

The sting of antiseptic on my shoulder makes me hiss in a breath and tense under Finn's fingers. He pauses, and a small flask appears in front of me. "Drink this," he murmurs. I take it from him and try to ignore the sound of him opening and prepping a suture kit while I hastily swallow some of the brandy. It's hot and smooth as it slides down my throat, leaving a flare of fire behind it before it fades into a pleasant numbed warmth.

The first stab of the needle whips through me, and I scream involuntarily. Finn fists a hand in my hair, pulling me back against him, a hand clamped over my mouth, and I bite it off, swallowing down the agony, the scream. The pain recedes under the feeling of his arms around me, until that is all I can feel—that and the warmth of the brandy, sitting like a lit coal in my belly.

"*Be quiet,*" Fin hisses in my ear, and my panic fades in the face of fury. I elbow him in the gut, even angrier when he releases me without comment.

"I told you, keep your hands off me, O'Malley," I say, but my voice is shaky and weak, and he laughs.

"Do I need to gag you?" he asks, his question sliding across my skin. I shiver.

I shake my head, and he smiles—I feel it where his lips are almost pressed against my skin. Fury floods me, hot and choking, and my cheeks flame. "You can curse me after, Nurrin. For now, hold still."

It's one of the hardest things I've ever done, but I manage it. He watches me for a few seconds when he comes around from behind my shoulder, his eyes slipping down to the lip I've bitten raw and the sweat that has beaded above it. Something shifts in his gaze, and he nods at the flask. "Take a little more, Nurrin."

I swallow two large gulps, clench my fist, and nod. He gives me a faint smile, ducks his head, and begins. Twice, I whimper, and he pauses, letting me gather myself, drink some more of the brandy. Once, he stops and wipes away the blood trailing down my chin. His gentleness is unnerving. I shift, moving slightly away from him.

He doesn't stop again, and stabbing burn, followed by a sharp tug, repeated over and over, makes me want to gag as he closes the wound.

When he's finally done, Finn lets out a deep breath. He stands, washing his hands quickly in the bathroom then coming back and throwing a bottle of pills onto the bed next to me. "Antibiotics," he says. "Neural inhibitors."

"What the hell are you doing with these?" I demand. "The CDC controls them."

He gives me a cold look, and I roll my eyes. "That's right. Finn O'Malley, man of mystery and endless questions. Why would I think you'd answer a simple question?"

"Answering questions wasn't part of this," he says, stripping off his shirt. My mouth goes dry. "You wanted to come, you'll do it blind—I don't believe in answering questions."

I stand. "What *do* you believe in, O'Malley? From what I see, the only thing you believe in is yourself and my brother."

And that bothers me. It always will.

Finn pauses, hands on his belt, and cocks an eyebrow at me. "Does it matter? I'll keep you alive. I'll keep Collin safe. And I'll get Dustin's meds. Beyond that, does it matter?"

He hesitates, watching me, and I finally shake my head, because he's right. It doesn't. Something flickers in his gaze, before it's gone and he nods. Then he slips into the bathroom, and I curl on my side, trying to sleep despite my racing thoughts.

When he comes out of the bathroom, Finn is wearing a pair of low-slung pajama bottoms and nothing else. He throws his clothes into the corner of the room and wordlessly crawls into the bed.

I almost land on my ass in my haste to scramble out of the bed.

Finn doesn't even turn on, but his voice floats out of the darkness. "Get a shower and get some sleep, Nurrin."

"I'm not sleeping with you," I say, my voice shrill.

That does make him move, and his lips twist into a sinful smile as he peers at me over his shoulder. "Are you sure?"

My mouth goes dry, and I breathe a curse on a shaky voice. He laughs and settles back on his side of the bed. "Sleep in the bed or the on the ground—I don't care."

His laughter follows me, faintly amusing, into the shower.

I end up sleeping in the bed. The floor is too hard, and the lure of a good night of sleep outweighs the distaste of sleeping next to Finn.

I can feel the steady pressure of his gaze in the morning. It's what wakes me—the warmth of the sunshine on my hair and his gaze on my face. I lie still, pretending to sleep, and for some reason, he lets me.

Finn O'Malley, who tolerates no dissembling or lies.

I relax a little when he slips from the bed, and I listen to him move around the small room then the sound of his feet on the stairs. The fresh scent of clean air hits me, and I groan, stretching. My stitches tug a little, in time with my throbbing head.

There's a hitch in his steps, and I listen, trying to figure out what he's doing. A sharp, antiseptic smell stings my nose, and I sit up abruptly, my feet swinging to the ground.

Bleach and antibacterial disinfectant—industrial grade. The smell is familiar; it's sprayed on the walls of the Haven every morning and mid-afternoon. It's a scent as familiar as my own, as familiar as home.

It's a zombie repellent.

He creeps back down the stairs, pulling the door shut with a soft snick, and wets the towel from last night's shower with the solution before shoving it under the door.

I'm trying not to shake when he finally stops, his eyes meeting mine. I see what he'll say.

We're trapped.

Chapter 19

Forced Together

I sit on the bed while he dresses in the bathroom. My arm is throbbing and I wish I hadn't turned down the pain pills Finn offered. Nerves flutter in my belly as the door to the bathroom opens and he steps out. He drops onto the bed. It squeaks, alarmingly loud in the silence. I wonder if we can be heard, or if the zombies have lost interest by now.

"How long will they stay?"

Finn glances at me, gray eyes piercing. I shiver. He shrugs and tugs on his second boot. "Could be gone already, or they could stay out there for another four hours. They could keep us here all day."

I cross my arms and glare at him. "We have to get to 18."

"Yes, Nurrin, I am aware of your thoughts on the matter. Give me your arm."

Because it's killing me—certainly not because he told me to—I do. He unwraps the bandage quickly, and we both can see the angry line of infection spreading from the wound. It looks like hell, and I can almost feel the disease infecting me. I yank my arm away. He lets me, tension filling him.

"Did you take the neural inhibitors?" Finn asks, his voice dangerous, and I bite my lip. "Mother*fuck,* Ren!" he snarls, and I flinch away as he jerks to his feet. He digs in his pack, pulling out another dose and thrusting them at me.

"Take them."

I bat his hand away. Neural inhibitors are a last resort, and they don't work as often as they do. "No way in hell."

The words have barely left my lips when he has me on my back, my hands caught in his. I gasp at the pressure of his body on mine, and something flares in his eyes. He makes a noise in the back of his throat.

I bring my knee up sharply and he laughs as he rolls away then pins my legs with one of his. I'm caught, neatly splayed beneath him, and I hate it.

"Take them."

"Screw you," I spit.

He shifts a little, and my eyes widen. A grim smile twists his lip. "It's one way to spend the day, Nurrin."

I don't respond. Something—a tiny voice of practicality—tells me pushing him right now could land me in a place I don't want to be.

His eyes are mocking. "Take your medicine like a good girl, and I might let you go."

"They don't work. And I don't want to be a veg."

"These work. No side effects."

I shake my head, stubbornly, my fear of the pills more than my fear of Finn. I've heard too many tales of neural inhibitors attacking the brain instead of the infection. I'd rather he shoot me than turn into one of those mindless souls.

Sure they were harmless—they didn't want to eat everyone they met—but there was nothing there. The year I graduated from high school, I spent a summer working in Hellspawn's hospital. Caring for them was the worst part of the assignment, even worse than putting down an infect.

"Ren." His voice snaps me out of my mounting panic and back to him. "I promise. I've taken them. You won't become a veg."

Something in his voice—and because he has never lied to me before—makes me nod. He eases up a little, shifting to grab the bag without actually letting me up.

I gag when he drops them on my tongue, and Finn leans down, kissing me.

I swallow in surprise.

His lips don't leave mine, and he drops down on me completely as he takes my head in his large hands, nibbling at my lips. And despite the fact that it's Finn, it's a helluva kiss. Without conscious thought, I kiss him back. His tongue licks at my lips, and I open for him, whimpering a little as his tongue sweeps inside, twisting with mine and—

He rolls off me abruptly, sitting on the edge of the bed. "Good."

"Wha?"

Finn glances at me, cool and disinterested, and my face flames. "That was to get me to take the damn pills?"

"What did you think it was?" he answers, dripping disdain.

I don't answer. Instead, I kick him off the bed, jerk the blankets up around me, and ignore his laughter as my face burns.

Chapter 20

On the Road

I'm driving.

Not because he wanted me to, but because we both know we're short on time. Collin is trapped in that cave with a live infection, and we lost precious time on that damn boat. The sun sets, and we're still hours from Haven 18, so he hands me the keys and I slide into the seat that still holds Finn's body heat and scent. He pauses outside the car, and I wrinkle my nose at the sound of him peeing.

A moment later, he slams the door. "A pack of infects headed this way."

Without a word, I hit the gas, and we're back on the road. I glance at him as he shifts a few times in his seat, drumming his fingers nervously. "Problem, O'Malley?"

His lips twitch, and for a heartbeat I can feel them again. Then he shrugs. "I like control, Nurrin. Giving that up is hard."

I focus on the road. "Is that why you don't answer questions? Because you have to control what people know about you?"

"What makes you think I don't? It could be just you I refuse to answer."

I laugh. "You don't care enough to single me out. Besides, the girls in the Hive talk, you know. Everyone knows you don't answer questions."

"Then why do you persist in asking them?"

"Glutton for punishment?"

There is a faint amusement in his voice when he slouches in his seat and says, "Just drive, Nurrin. Quit asking questions you know I won't answer."

He closes his eyes, relaxed and ceding control enough to doze as I steer us through the star-studded night. I see zombies in the distance, loping along, pulled by the sound of our car. Once, we pass a convoy—five beat up RV's barreling through the night, lights blazing, three snipers on the roofs. I pull off the road when I see them coming, and one of the snipers waves at me, looking bored and tired as they race the night.

I wonder how many people were packed into the RV's.

Traveling between Havens is dangerous and expensive—I'd guess four or five families were crammed into each RV , splitting the exorbitant price as best they could.

"Get going, Nurrin," Finn says beside me. "And keep an eye out—that convoy will have a trail of dead."

He's right.

We hit the horde ten minute after passing the convoy, a small pack, but more than we can push through in the Porsche.

I idle on the road, staring at Finn as he stares at the approaching zombies, and I wonder what he's thinking.

"Give me you guns. Your bow, too."

I grab them from below my legs, and he slides himself up to perch on the window of the car.

"Keep it steady, Nurrin. I'll clear a path, but you have to get us through it."

His voice drifts through the window of the car. "Take it easy, but get some speed, Ren. Get us through this."

He's trusting me. And he just called me Ren. I grit my teeth and ease my foot on the accelerator. From the corner of my eye, I can see the wind pulling at his shirt as we gain speed. The first gunshot makes me flinch, and the car serves a little. He slams a hand on the roof. "Keep it straight, Nurrin!" he snarls.

I tune him out as we drive into the horde. They're moaning, racing at us from the darkness, and in two heartbeats, we're enveloped. There are enough to block off the road, but Finn does what he promised—the road stays clear. His shots have slowed, and I'm not sure if it's because he's low on ammo or because he's aiming, but either way, we need to get clear.

I call, "Hold on."

"Ren!" he shouts, and I grab one of his legs as I drive the pedal down. The Porsche roars under my touch, fishtailing a little before it shoots into the gap he's created. I feel him slip, and I almost slow down, but there are too many infects. Closing in from every direction. He fires twice, and the path opens, a brief window.

I take it, darting through. We burst from the horde into the empty night. Finn slides into the car, steadily cursing as he reaches into his bag.

He comes up with a hand grenade.

"Where the hell did that come from?" I demand, my voice shrill.

"What did I tell you about questions, Nurrin? Get this piece of shit moving." He pulls the pin, leans out the window, and lobs it into the midst of the zombies who have turned to chase us.

Finn is leaning back, his eyes closed, when the blast lights up the night sky and shakes the car. I glance into the rear view mirror, at the remains of the horde.

"Why didn't you do that to begin with?" I ask, glancing at him. He looks bloody, but it's fetid and old—blood splatter from the zoms he put down.

"We couldn't drive through an explosion," Finn says, without opening his eyes. "Stop staring. I didn't get bitten."

I flush, my gaze going back to the road. He laughs a little, says something softly under his breath. "What?" I snap.

"We won't be in Haven 18 long, but you can probably take care of that itch there."

"Oh, shut up, Finn. You have no idea."

He moves quickly, his lips brushing against my ear, sucking lightly on my earlobe before tracing the curve with his tongue. I shiver and he laughs. "I know if *I* can get that response, you are pretty desperate to get laid. I'd offer, but—"

"Fuck. You," I spit and he laughs.

"Yeah, that's what I thought you might say," he says, closing his eyes. Fuming, hating that desire is coiling in my belly, I ignore him and drive through the dying night.

Chapter 21

Answers and Questions

Haven 18 is nestled in the curve of the Rockies and sprawls before us like a glittering gem as I come around the crest of the mountain. Finn stirs, rubbing his eyes. "Pull off at the next outlook. I'll drive us in."

I glance at him, but don't say anything as we begin our descent, twisting through the pre-dawn light.

At the outlook, he glances over my clothes with a critical eye, and I flush. I don't look pretty. I look, more than anything, like I've spent the past several days in the Wide Open, killing zombies.

We don't get stopped until we're a mile from the wall, where a group of soldiers stand in the road like a miniature army.

He pulls up to them and lowers his window.

"Name and haven?" the general barks.

"Finn O'Malley and Nurrin Sanders, of Haven 8."

The man frowns, and I'm not sure if it's because of Finn's distinct accent or my name. "Last word from 8 was there was a breach," he says

"It fell," Finn says flatly, and the soldiers behind him suck in a sharp breath. "I have clearance to enter this haven, so if you'd let me pass..." he trails off.

The general sneers at him. "Whose clearance is that, boy?"

I can feel the tension that wraps around him, and I almost feel sorry for the older man. Being on the receiving end of Finn's glare when it goes dangerous and still is not something I'd wish on anybody.

Although, I am grateful it's turned on someone other than me.

He pulls something out of the door of the car, extending it without word, and the general glances at it half-heartedly. Then he looks back, his eyes wide and afraid.

"Do you have more questions?" Finn asks, coldly.

"No, sir. Apologies."

"Call ahead to the gate. I'm tired and want to get to my damn house."

I look at him sharply, but he's back in the *ignore Ren* mode. I peer at whatever he gave the general, but it's tucked away too quickly for me to see anything other than a flash of red. The guards clear the road, and we drive on toward the haven.

"Why did they let us pass?"

Finn glances at me. "When we get to the Haven, we're going straight to my house. I have a contact here. He'll come look at your arm. How are you feeling?"

"I thought you said there were no side effects."

He shrugs. "I've been known to lie before, Nurrin."

I swallow the curse, knowing it'll only amuse him. Instead I shake my head and settle back against the seat. "I feel fine, *sir*."

He grins and looks over at me. "That sounds particularly nice, coming from you."

This time I do curse, and his laughter is still ringing in my ears when we pull up to the gates. They glide open, and we drive through, the reek of zom repellent mixing with the scent of humanity, mountain air, and fruit ready to be harvested.

A medic is standing with the walkers, her little hands clasped over her kit. "I need to test both of you," she says, with a quick apologetic look at me. I shrug. It's standard procedure, and if the inhibitors worked, it shouldn't be an issue.

If they didn't, I'd rather be put down here.

Finn tenses, but doesn't object. Whatever got us this far won't get us out of a blood test.

She swabs his arm first, drawing a quick sample and injecting a specialized dye. The blood doesn't shift color, and I feel myself relax—he's clean.

Immediately, I hate that I care.

She runs the same test on me, and I look away as the dye sinks in, waiting for it to latch into the virus swimming in my blood. Finn is staring at the vial, his expression tight. I can't read the expression in his eyes, but it makes my nerves sing. Then he relaxes, and I look at the vial the medic is holding.

Dark red.

Finn clenches my hand before I can say anything, and he talks to the Walkers briefly before we're waved through.

He drives without hesitation, and I wonder when he was here last.

The house is on a quiet street, clean and unassuming and well maintained.

"Come on," he orders, killing the engine and grabbing our bags. I shelve my questions and scramble out of the car to follow him inside.

It's strange, to be exposed on the street and not be concerned about infects. Being in the Wide Open left a mark, faster than I thought it would.

The house is dark and barren. A few pieces of furniture in the great room and a single picture on the wall of the hallway.

It's the space that really startles me.

Havens have a limit of space. Most residents are crammed into vast apartment complexes, tiny lofts shared by whole families. But this—this is a two bedroom *house* with a surplus of space, and he doesn't even live here.

It might be time, I realize, to reassess what I know about the mysterious man who befriended my brother.

"Lee will be here soon." Finn says, tossing our bags onto the couch. "You can take a shower, if you want."

I stare at him, and for a long moment, he stares back. Questions are racing through my head, and he's watching me. Daring me to ask them. I take a deep breath. "Sounds great."

Amusement tilts his lips, a little, before he turns to lead me into the bathroom. As I pass him, he inhales, his emotions flashing across his face before he shuts them down and leaves me.

When I emerge from my shower, my hair smells clean for the first time in days. My clothes are a bit dusty, but I don't mind too much, and I pad barefoot down the hall, finger combing my hair.

Finn is standing in the kitchen with a young man.

He's heavier than Finn, thick in a way that screams weight lifter. His hair is girlishly long, a burnished red, and pale blue eyes skim over me in interest.

"You brought a girl to your home?" he asks, surprise evident in his tone.

"No questions," Finn intervenes, his gaze darting to me and daring me to say something. I shrug and sit down. "You're the doctor, I presume."

Lee nods—it's a safe question. "He said your arm and shoulder had exposure."

I extend my arm, and Lee comes around to examine it. His head bends over me, his long hair tickling my skin, and I idly wonder if it's as soft as it looks.

I glance up when Finn moves. He's still standing in the kitchen, leaning back against the counter with his arms crossed over his chest.

His eyes are stormy as he watches us, and I must make a noise, something that draws his gaze from Lee's hands on my stitches to meet my own.

For a moment, his gaze is hot, furious, so full of emotions it makes my mouth go dry. I lick my lips, and his gaze drops to my mouth. Hunger flares in his eyes, unmistakable.

"What caused this?"

The question jars me; I flush and look away as Finn's face goes blank.

"We had an incident—she was clawed by an infect."

"How recently?"

"Thirty two hours."

Lee frowns. "It's remarkably clear. Most cases, I'd recommend Q."

"I don't have time for that," I blurt before I can stop myself. Lee raises his eyebrows.

"You aren't testing for infection, and the wound is clean. Keep long sleeves on to avoid questions, but you'll do."

Finn straightens, coming to stand by the couch, and I feel like I've taken my first deep breath in days.

They talk for a few minutes, but I'm lost in my thoughts and relief.

The door closes, and Finn reenters the room. He glides past me. I wonder if I should say something.

"It was the neural inhibitors."

My words stop him, and he stands in the hallway, his back to me.

"If you had them, why didn't you give them to Dustin?"

He laughs. The bastard actually laughs at me. "Nurrin, neural inhibitors are regulated. Getting them is ridiculously expensive."

I glance around the house. "You have unoccupied *houses* and can call a doctor to them in the middle of the night with no advance warning. Clearly, money is not an issue."

His eyes sparkle. "Some things stretch even my budget."

"This could have saved him," I say, ignoring his amusement. I feel cold, shocked. Does Dustin's life mean nothing?

Finn answers the question I hadn't realized I voiced. "I told you in the Hive. He's your baggage, Nurrin. I allowed him to come to get you to shut up, and because Collin wouldn't leave without you. I don't *care* if he survives."

"Then why bother giving them to me?" I snap and jerk to my feet

He catches my arm as I stride by him, pulling me around until I'm facing him. I glare at a spot on his chest, refusing to look into his gaze.

One of his hands fists in my hair, tilting my head back until I'm staring at him. I should be spitting mad—but there it is. The same hunger I saw in him when Lee was working on my arm, smoldering in his eyes now. I lick my lips as heat pools between my legs and his gaze heats.

"Do you really want me to apologize for that?" he murmurs, and I feel the brush of his breath against my lips. "Do you expect me to apologize for keeping you alive? Because if you do, you're a damn fool. And I always thought you were smart, Ren."

I shake my head, as much as his grip will allow. "You never thought about me at all."

Something fills his gaze, something more dangerous than lust, and I hold my breath. Then he releases his grip on my hair. Blood rushes through my scalp, tiny pinpricks of pain as he steps away from me. "Go to bed, Nurrin."

I want to call him on it—the name he uses to distance himself from me, all the secrets, the desire he's barely keeping leashed. I open my mouth, but he cuts me off, "I swear to god, Ren. You don't want to do this. Go."

My mouth closes with a click, and I spin, marching into a bedroom—his—and shutting the door behind me. I pause, hear his footsteps on the other side of the wood, and reach down to lock it.

Chapter 22

Day One

The door creaks open, and I lift the cross bow as Finn enters. Two steps and *twang.*

He freezes as the quarrel hits right in front of him, buried in the wall.

Finn stares at the quivering fletching for a moment then looks at me. "Something wrong, Nurrin?"

"Where the fuck have you been?" I snarl, finally letting the crossbow drop.

When I emerged from the bedroom this morning, I'd been startled to find the house empty. He left a note, ordering me to stay put. And I'd been happy enough to do so—I searched the house for any information about Finn, but aside from the single framed picture, there was nothing personal about the house.

And the picture told me nothing—just two men walking under some trees, each holding a child's hand.

When my search yielded nothing, I tried to leave. And found all the doors locked. The bastard had actually locked me *in* the damn house.

He looks around now, taking in the trashed living room. His eyebrows raise a little, and the look he gives me is a mixture of amused irritation. "I had things to do. We came here for a reason, remember?"

"So you locked me in the house? That doesn't strike you as, I don't know, *fucking insane*?"

He shrugs. "It kept you safe and out of trouble. That's all that really matters to me."

"We're in a Haven," I shout. "It's perfectly safe."

He moves then, across the room, crowding into my personal space. I squeak as he leans into me, backing me up into the chair.

"It's Day One, and you're a first. In a strange Haven with no protection. You know what they do to Firsts, Nurrin. Be pissy. Destroy the house. I don't give a fuck. I won't let you put yourself in danger because you want some fresh air."

It's Day One. I count the days in my head, backing up until I realize he's right. It's my birthday, the day the zombies rose.

He's watching me. "Did you want to be out there, alone?"

Dread tickles my belly, and I have to shake my head.

Being a First—firstborn after the dead came back—came with its own set of issues. Including the cult that sprang up during the change. I shake my head, trying to dislodge the memory, painfully aware that he's watching me.

"Can you wake me up next time?" I ask, my voice low. "Take me with you."

I look up and see the sardonic tilt to his lips. "I didn't realize you'd want to be with me," he drawls.

I'm too tired for this—for his games and subtle rebuffs, for the disdain he oozes when he looks at me.

"You know, I don't have time for this," I say, standing. "I don't care if you don't want me here—if you'd rather it was Collin. I came here to get the medicine to help my boyfriend. Medicine you neglected to mention you had. You do whatever you have to do, O'Malley, but don't stop me from doing what I came for."

I turn to walk away then say over my shoulder, "I'm going tomorrow, to get what I need. Help me or stay out of my way. But don't try to stop me."

Finn catches me at my bedroom door. He pulls me to a stop, and I look up at him. I don't know what I expect to see there—disgust, amusement, irritation, hunger. I don't ever know what to expect with him. And that fascinates me.

"It's your birthday, Nurrin."

I flinch, looking away as tears pool in my eyes. That is the last thing I expect to hear. "No. It's Day One."

He pushes my hair from my face, a gesture so gentle it makes my breath stop, and my eyes are wide and confused when I look at him. His gaze is so full I can't decipher what I see there.

If I were very honest, I would admit that I don't *want* to decipher what I see there. But I am rarely that honest.

"Day One is the day our whole world changed. But it's also the day a girl was born. A girl who deserves to be known for more than just being a first." I gasp, and his hand drops away, leaving a searing heat in its wake. "I see that girl."

"Why are you saying this?" I demand, and I'm not even sure what I'm asking. His gaze heats and he turns away.

"Be ready at nine. I have an appointment."

Fuck. That. I want one answer. One damned answer. I catch him and yank on his arm.

He moves faster than I expect, his body pushing against mine, holding me captive against the door, his lips hard on mine. I gasp and, with a groan, he sweeps into my mouth, sucking softly on my tongue. Something deep inside me clenches, a hungry yearning.

I whimper, and he shifts, all of his weight bracing me, and the press of him against my belly, hard and impatient, makes me squirm anxiously.

His mouth leaves mine, trailing kisses on my neck. When he bites down on my earlobe, I almost faint.

I make a noise, and he groans, the noise vibrating against my skin. Pulls back and stares at me with hot, hungry eyes.

"Does that answer any of your questions?" he murmurs before be backs away from me, leaving me empty and aching and cold.

It doesn't. It answers nothing. I go into my room, strip, and crawl into his bed alone, with more questions than he will ever answer.

When I wake, the blanket is tucked around me and light is streaming into the room through the safety bars. I can hear Finn moving through the house, and I sit up, reaching for my shirt.

At the end of my bed is a folded pair of leather pants, a corset, and heels. And a small box, with a simple black ribbon on the top. I pick up the note and read it quickly.

Wear the clothes. Collin would want you to have something on your birthday.

F-

I open the box and stare at my gun.

It's so familiar it looks out of place there, the familiar little gun I've carried for so many years. The gun that Mom carried before me.

The gun I lost in the wide open, protecting Finn.

The wild thought goes through me—when did he get it? Had he had it all along? He must have.

And then, the realization that has taken a long time to set in.

Finn was in my room, while I slept.

Part 2

The Boy Without a Past

*

If the past was what we were meant to see. Then behind, not in front, our eyes would be.

Author Unknown

**

The past means nothing—it died the same day the dead rose.

Finn O'Malley

Chapter 1

Old Friend

She's wearing them when she emerges from my bedroom.

Her blonde hair is pulled back, exposing every inch of her face and neck. The pants fit her like a second skin, displaying her lush ass. The black corset is laced up tight, pushing her small breasts together and up.

For a split second, I can't think about anything but pushing her against the wall and licking every inch of her delicious skin.

Then she pulls out the gun.

I swallow my desire and raise a lazy eyebrow. "Drawing on me again, Nurrin?"

"Where did you get it?" she demands.

"You dropped it during the flat."

I knew what that gun meant to her. She might not see it, but I have watched her for years. Waiting. Hoping like hell the urge to fuck her would go away.

It never did.

But I learned about her—and I knew damn well what that gun meant. Her eyes soften a little, and I straighten. "Get your coffee—we're late."

And just like that, the softness is gone, replaced with curiosity.

I hand her a leather jacket and lead the way from the house.

"Where are we going?" She shuts the door of the Porsche to punctuate her question, and I grit my teeth.

"Does it ever occur to you that asking me questions is an exercise in futility?"

She grins, mischievous. "Nope."

A slow smile tilts my lips. Her eyes drop down and get that sleepy, sexy look that never fails to make me a little hard. I jerk the car into motion, and she gets thrown against her seat. I hear her curse.

And hide my grin.

"I don't know, Finn. Your evidence is thin."

Nurrin shifts at my side, and Lissel spares her a brief look. It's killing her to stay quiet, but so far Nurrin has managed to follow my orders.

"So you won't evacuate the Haven?" I ask.

Lissel shakes her head. "It's too much. And the Wide Open is dangerous—we'll take our chances here."

I nod. "Fine."

Nurrin makes a surprised noise, and Lissel smiles, the knowing smile that first intrigued me and now just makes me want to slap her. "You will be here long?" she asks, her hand lingering on my arm.

I glance down at it, at the fingers I've seen on my cock while her blonde hair spread across my thighs.

Now I stare at her until two spots of color appear in her cheeks and she pulls away. "No," I answer shortly.

"You have nowhere to go. Haven 8 is gone."

I laugh at that and stand. Nurrin leaps to her feet, twitching with impatience. "Lissel, you know better. I always have *somewhere* to go."

Nurrin laughs softly, and Lissel's sharp gaze goes to her. "She's a First."

It isn't a question. I straighten slowly and shrug. "So?"

"The Order would be thrilled to hear a First is in the Haven. And so close to Third Day, too."

I move before I think, pin Lissel to the door, my knee braced between her legs, my hand on her throat. Her eyes are amused and angry. Vaguely, I wonder if I have made the biggest mistake of my life.

"Finn," Nurrin hisses. I ignore her—I'm damn good at that.

I stare at Lissel, letting a dangerous smile play on my lips. "If word spreads that she's a First, my life will become messy. You *know* I don't like messy."

Her eyes narrow, and I shake her a little. "Don't push this, Lissel. I don't want to kill you."

Blue eyes widen and behind me I hear Nurrin gasp. "Go to the car," I snap. For a long moment, she hesitates, and I almost yell at her. Then the door opens, snicks softly closed.

I release Lissel abruptly, and she stumbles. "What the hell are you doing?" I snarl. She stares at me unrepentant, and I turn away, disgusted.

"Don't play games with me. I'll kill you and be done with them."

If there is any response, I don't hear it above the door I slam shut behind me.

Nurrin is watching me, her eyes full of accusations and questions. I shift, feeling the gears of the Porsche grinding, and grit my teeth. Turn sharply. Nurrin yelps as she tumbles toward me. For a heartbeat, her skin is pressed against me, her scent all around me.

I shrug her off, and she retreats to her side of the car. "Can you drive like a sane person?" she grumbles.

"Can you put a seat belt on?"

"Where are we going?"

The endless fucking questions. I think I could handle all of the reasons why fucking Ren is the worst idea in a long line of bad ideas—if it weren't for the endless fucking questions. I ignore her, steering the Porsche through the quiet streets of Haven.

I like 18. Always have. Maybe because I visited here, before the rising. Before the walls and the guns and the decay. I shut down that line of thought—it doesn't do any good to think of that time. It's over. It's been over for twenty years.

Shady trees shiver in the breeze floating off the ocean. A few women are clustered in a shop, bartering.

There are no children wandering Haven 18. Sometimes, there is such a lack of them, I start thinking the plague took them as well.

It's not true—our children are hidden deep in the Haven, behind every wall and defense we can manage, protected by the best guards, with three ways of escape in the event of a breach.

Not that it saved the children of Haven 8. Not that it will save them here.

But the defense measures make nervous mothers happy while their fathers Walk the walls.

Idiots. The idiots shouldn't breed if they're going to risk themselves like that—although, I don't see much point in it at all. Not in this world.

Although—fucking is fun. Maybe that is the point.

"Finn?"

Her voice is sharp and sweet and fills the confines of the car. I'm already surrounded by her scent and thinking of sex and all of it makes me want to pull over, drag her onto my lap, and sink into her until she's screaming.

I slide a look at her—she looks irritated. Whatever she sees in my eyes makes her pale, lick her lips. I wonder if she's thinking of the kiss.

I wonder how long I can make myself wait before I kiss her again.

"Fuck," I growl, jerking my eyes forward again.

The car grumbles under me, and I turn sharply. She curses and I smirk—I love hearing her curse. One of the best things about her is that she curses so damn well.

"Stop doing that," she grumbles. I ease the car to a stop in front of a small house and kill the engine.

"Wait here," I order, stepping out of the car. There's maybe a twenty-five percent chance she'll listen to me.

Her door slams shut behind me, and I throw her a glare. "Don't waste your breath," she mutters as she comes along side me. In her heels, she's as tall as I am. And gorgeous, all sex and leather. I catch her arm. "Same rules, Nurrin. Mouth shut and do what I tell you."

"Who are we seeing?"

I start walking again, striding up to the little house. I can smell the oil and paint, pungent and mixing with the zombie repellent that soaks the haven.

Jesse grins when he opens the door. I nod briefly, stepping past him. I see the flash of curiosity in his eyes a heartbeat before he stifles it. His attention swivels back to me, professional and doing his damned best to ignore the impatient, curious girl radiating sex.

I wonder if I can kill him for looking at her.

Would be a hassle—finding a good mechanic in the western havens is never easy. But if she says anything to encourage the interest in his eyes, I'll break his fucking neck.

The thought amuses me, and a smile twitches my lip. "Sit down, Nurrin."

Jesse's eyes widen, and I shift, slightly. Shielding her. He's never had ties to the Order, but trusting Ren's safety to anyone but Collin is impossible. Hell, trusting Collin with her is hard.

"The Porsche looks like shit. What did you do to it?" Jesse ask, breaking the tension.

At the table, Ren laughs. I don't turn to her, don't drink in the smile that's curving her kissable lips. "The Wide Open didn't agree with it. Can you get it cleaned up?"

"To your standards?"

I shake my head. The car was flawed— attempting to restore it to what it was is a waste of time. "Find a buyer."

Nurrin shifts, and I step away from her. "How is the Harley?"

Jesse's gaze slides over Ren, and I glance back at her. She's smiling, a fuck-me tilt to the lips, her eyes sleepy.

"She's not really dressed for the bike, Finn."

"She's none of your damn concern," I snap, and her eyes flick to me, amused. "Get the bike. I'll meet you in the garage."

There's a moment of hesitation from Jesse, but he's used to following orders, and he knows my temper. He leaves.

"What the fuck are you doing?" I ask without looking at her.

She moves, standing lithely. I stay very still as she comes up behind me, her breath whispering over my skin as she says, "Scratching an itch."

I grab her as she struts away. Her eyes are filled with amusement and a challenge. "No."

An eyebrow arches, and she laughs. "Why not?"

My jaw clenches, and something flickers in her gaze. Disgust.

Why did I have to obsess over the girl who couldn't be happy with a good fuck? Why the one who needed to know *everything*.

I release her. "Fine. Scratch away. Have him bring you home—and my bike."

She opens her mouth to say something— probably ask another bloody question—but I ignore it, ignore her yelling my name as I leave.

Chapter 2

Killing Aggression

Every Haven has a Wall. And every wall needs Walkers. I stalk there now, ignoring the curious faces of Haven citizens, the mourning incense still hanging like a pungent cloud over the city.

There is very little I dislike more than Day One and the subsequent days. She's at her most vulnerable then. For a heartbeat, I hesitate. Leaving her with Jesse is making all of my protective instincts scream. But I kissed her last night—if I keep up with the over-protective alpha-male routine, she'll bolt. I make a face. This long game might be worth the end reward, but there's something to be said for instant gratification. Namely, that it's instant.

There are a few Walkers in the barracks, and I nod at them. "Help you?" one asks.

I smile lazily. "Haven 8. Chief Walker of the Western sector."

"Bit far from your sector, sir," he says, politely questioning my right to be here.

I hate questions. Despise them. Why don't people get that questions are just a way to lie. The answers don't mean anything—they aren't earned, they're given for nothing. How could they mean anything? "Just need a bit of a distraction. Do you mind?"

He eyes me for a moment then shrugs. "A Walker's a Walker, no matter where he hails. Try not to get yourself killed up there."

I flash a sharp smile, but don't say anything in response. He steps aside, and I jog up the steep stairs.

The Wall is twenty feet thick, a hundred feet high. On the inside, it's braced by buildings and barracks, small businesses that cater to the thrill-seekers.

On the outside, there is nothing. A sheer, smooth drop directly to the ground, no vegetation or growth sprouting along the Wall. No trees within fifty yards. It's like a great big hand carved away all of nature's beauty and dropped a fortified city in its place.

It gleams white in the morning light, the stink of zom repellent still filling the air. It's a familiar scent, on the Wall. Almost as familiar as the scent of blood and decay.

I see a small herd milling around a fallen deer. Infects prefer humans—if they can get at a healthy human, they'll bypass any wild game for a shot at spreading the disease. But when hungry and desperate enough, they aren't terribly picky.

Any meat will do when they're starving.

Aside from the infects feeding, it's a quiet morning—the border is empty. I lean against the wall, my finger tapping incessantly. This isn't what I need. I'm too edgy, anxious. "Do you have a patrol scheduled?"

The Walker at my left shifts, surprised. "Sir?"

I flick my head, annoyed. "A patrol. Scouting parties."

He stares at me blankly, and I growl, clattering down the stairs and approaching the fortified gate. It's a stone door that slides directly into place, which lets Walkers into the Wide Open to patrol beyond the Haven and clear the wall.

"I'm going out," I say, digging into their armory and finding a crossbow and a wicked-sharp axe. It's a personal weapon, one that requires close quarters. It's perfect. Now I just need an infect. "Open the gate."

"Sir, you can't go out there," one of the Walkers objects.

I give him a long look, and he finally flushes, looking down. "Open. The gate," I repeat flatly.

There's a screeching sound of metal on metal, and a narrow gap appears. I slip through it, putting the gleaming white of the wall behind me. The open air teases my skin, carrying the scent of wild pine and infects.

"You're crazy, you know."

I glance sideways at the Walker who followed me out of the Haven. I give a tight smile, and then a low moan draws my attention.

The herd with the deer has caught our scent, and one's head is whipping around, her moan an angry call as she searches. I pull my bow up, slowly, and carefully draw the string back. There's a sharp twang, which draws the others' attention. Then the quarrel catches her in the forehead, spinning her around as she falls.

"Incoming," I say, and the Walker shoots me a disbelieving look—the amusement in my voice has to disturb him. The zombies take all my attention, and for the first time since I left the Hole, I'm not thinking about her. I'm not thinking about anything but the arrow I'm aiming, the putrid body bag bolting across the clearing toward me, and the axe in my hand as I swing it around. The zombie screams just before my blade slices into its neck, and I smile, a mad hatter grin, as I go to work.

The scream draws more—five infects burst from the tree line at a dead sprint as the Walker puts down the last of the first pack. I hiss—I'm tired and running low on arrows—before jerking the crossbow up and taking aim. I drop three, and the Walker picks off a fourth. As I line up the sights of the fifth, I hesitate—her long blonde hair is still shiny, her face almost untouched by the infection. She's new and furious, awkward with the disease rampant in her blood system. The ends of her gold hair are bloody.

She reminds me, for a heartbeat, of the past. I close my eyes and squeeze the trigger, breathing out as the bow bucks slightly. I hear the muffled thud of the body, finally dead, hitting the ground. Sudden exhaustion sweeps me as I survey the carnage—it was senseless risk, and I'm sure I'll hear all kinds of shit from Lissel later. But it did what I needed, until that last biter. A little annoyed that she ruined my high, I stalk around the dead, ripping arrows from their skulls. The

Walker paces alongside me, eyeing me as he keeps watch.

"Have something to say?" I finally ask, bored. I jerk another arrow free and take the gore covered bolts back toward the Wall.

"We all have our ways of dealing with the Turn."

I stare at him, a smile ticking my lips up. He pales. The fucker shot down a rampaging horde, took point while I retrieved shit we could do without—and a smile from me makes him nervous.

I don't address his statement, the truth in it— or the fact that this isn't a yearly blowup.

This is my life—everyone's—every day.

Chapter 3

Cleaning Up

She's back. I know, even before I push open the front door, that she's back—the air feels slightly different when she's sharing it with me, a subtle tension fills it that only I seem to be aware of.

I take a deep breath and open the door, letting a blank expression fall over my face.

I don't need it—she's asleep, snoring slightly, curled on her side on the couch. A blanket has slipped off her, exposing the soft curves of her breast and ass, still encased in the outfit I gave her.

I start to walk past, and she make a little noise, halting me in my tracks.

Damn her for the ability to do that. I kick the couch, and she snaps upright, her gun trained on my head. I keep my face straight, despite the urge to grin. She's always ready for an attack. Collin trained her well—but then, he would. He's lost too much to risk his sister.

"The door was unlocked," I say, and she blinks, relaxing a tiny bit when she sees it's only me.

"I didn't think you had the keys," she answers, tossing them to me.

"It's dangerous for you to be unprotected right now," I say, looking away.

She's quiet, for so long I finally look back at her. She's staring at me, emotions spreading across her face too quickly for me to follow. Finally she smirks. "Didn't think you cared."

My own words, echoing back at me. A smile twitches my lips. "Collin would be pissed if anything happened to you, Nurrin."

She looks away. "Did you get the meds?"

I shrug out of my leather jacket, and she inhales sharply. I'm still covered in blood from the skirmish outside the Wall. "What happened?" she demands shrilly, taking a short step toward me. I pin her with a sharp look, and she stops.

I ignore her, pulling the bloody shirt of. It sticks to my chest. I grimace. "I'm going to shower," I announce, turning toward my bedroom.

"Finn O'Malley, you have to answer me," she snaps. "You have to talk to me!"

The bathroom feels crowded with her in it. I hook my thumbs in the top of my jeans, ready to shove them down. "You might want to leave," I murmur, turning to stare at her.

Her cheeks are flushed, but she sets her feet, crossing her arms. I grin, slow and amused. I unbutton and push my jeans down.

Her breath catches, her gaze skirting down before snapping up to my eyes. "I'm not leaving without answers, Finn."

I step into her space, so close I can feel the heat of her skin, the brush of her corset-clad breasts. "See something you like, little girl?"

"Nothing terribly impressive," she shoots back, and I laugh at that. Her breathing is fast, her eyes a little sleepy. She's primed for sex and a fight, and I want to give her both.

I lean into her, inhaling her scent and licking at her pounding pulse point. She shivers, swaying toward me. "You sure, Nurrin? It's gotta be more fun than taking care of yourself."

"Who says I did," she murmurs, and I jerk upright. "Jesse is quite talented. At many things."

I want to throttle him. Or her. Instead, I twist and turn on the shower. The water is scalding hot, and it stings my skin as I step into the spray, ignoring her completely.

Knowing she was with other men in Haven 8 I could handle—there was distance, and I slept around. Tried to get her out of my system. But here, it's somehow different. I want to strangle Jesse, push her against a wall and kiss her until she can't remember anyone's name but mine.

"You can't ignore me and expect me to wait for you to do whatever it is you're doing," she shouts over the spray. I fist my erection and turn to her, blatantly displaying myself. Her eyes widen, and she bites her lip.

"I can, actually. You'll listen or I'll lock you in until I'm ready to go back to the Hole."

She bares her teeth in a parody of a smile and turns away.

Fuck. "Nurrin!" I snarl, and jump out of the shower. She's almost to the door, moving fast, when I tackle her. She hits the ground with a yelp. I roll, pulling her under my wet, still-bloody body.

"Get off me, you bastard," she shouts, and I clamp down hard on her wrists as she reaches to slap me. I force her hand down and glare at her.

"Are you fucking insane? Or just *trying* to get yourself killed? The Order is out there, hunting Firsts. You *idiot.*"

"I don't care," she says, and I groan, letting my weight drop on her. She gasps, squeezing her eyes closed. "Dustin needs me. The longer you fuck around, the longer Collin is with that danger."

My stomach twists, and I pull away. "It's too dangerous to go out while the Turn is being remembered."

"That didn't stop you this morning. And it's too dangerous for Collin to wait."

She's right. She's right, and I can't do a damn thing about it. I prop myself up and stare at her. "You have to listen."

Hope sparks in her eyes, and she nods, a quick bob of her head. "Just like the Wide Open, Finn."

I roll off her, and she stays there for a minute, staring up at me. I don't look at her, just turn and stalk back to my abandoned shower.

Chapter 4

The Blessed Order

She strides alongside me on the quiet street. Mourning incense fills the air and my head, the streets taking on an eerie quality in the dimness. I glance at her from the corner of my eye. If she's nervous being on the streets during Second Night, she's doing a damn good job at hiding it.

She's dressed in a scarlet bandage dress with a black ribbon shoulder strap. Paired with her black stilettos, she looks sexy and dangerous and five years older than she is.

She doesn't look like a First.

"Where are we going?" she asks.

I roll my eyes, catch her elbow, and pull her along a little faster. She mutters darkly under her breath.

The building looks deserted, but according to Jesse, this is the best place to find what I need. The black market meds are going to be where every other vice in the Haven is found. Everything is controlled by one group.

I knock quickly and lean down to murmur into Nurrin's ear. "Quiet, little girl. Understand? Follow my lead."

She twitches and nods, just as the door swings open. I eye the bouncer, the steady thrum of music pounding behind him. "We're closed."

I pull out a bag full of narcotics and creds. His eyes widen, and I smirk. "Finn O'Malley, with a guest. Let me in."

The guard steps aside, and we go into the long, wide hallway that separates the main club from the door. "Stay to the middle," I say, dragging her close behind me.

"Why?" she asks, and an infect explodes into the room from the left. Nurrin chokes a scream down, a half-heard noise that's buried when she bites down on my shoulder. I grunt and keep walking—her hands clenched in the silk of my dress shirt.

The infect is harmless—as harmless as they ever are. His lower jaw has been shattered, teeth removed in a gaping maw. His fingers are broken off stubs, but the bone protrudes—enough to pick up a contact infection.

"Why?" she asks, again, her voice shaking and scared.

"They don't want anyone stumbling onto this," I answer. The zombie hisses at us, broken fingers stretched. She shudders, and I keep going down the hall.

Another bouncer is waiting, this one visibly armed. He levels a gun at us, and I feel fury building in me. I understand the precautions, but at some point, they just become offensive. I'm well past my limit for irritating shit.

I draw my own gun, cock it, and point at his forehead. "My bribe already paid our passage. Unless you want this place brought to the aldermen's attention, you'll put that down and let me fucking pass."

He smirks. "I heard O'Malley had graced the Haven again. Didn't expect to see you in the Underground."

"That's because you don't know a damn thing about me," I say coldly. The bouncer's eyes flick to Nurrin, and she shifts, a little bit away from me. I want to drag her back, but it'd cause questions I don't want to deal with.

He smiles and moves aside.

And we step into the Underground.

A dance floor has been set up in one half of the club—flashing lights and cheap beer is flowing, half-dressed girls dance on tables. A few couples are making out; one girl has her hand down her partner's pants, toying with his erection.

Nurrin watches curiously, but I turn her away. Between the dance floor and the stalls selling goods, is a bar. A few working girls linger there, watching me, and this time, Nurrin draws closer, almost jealously.

I lead her past the bar and the illegal black market, deeper into the heart of the Underground. Here there's a sexual playground, where any fetish and appetite can be satisfied. The music is replaced by low moans, the sound of chains rattling, and cries of pleasure—the scent of sex hangs on the air. Her eyes are wide when she looks at me, and I shake my head. A sub being whipped by a leather-clad domme watches with lazy, pleasure-hazed eyes as I lead Nurrin past the kink club.

There's another door, but this one is unmanned. I push it open, leading her into the fight pit.

Two men—a Walker and a Haven worker—are fighting. From the mess of their faces, they've been at it a while, but the crowd is still screaming, hysterical, driven by an urge for blood.

Nurrin watches for a few seconds as the Walker pummels the other man mercilessly. The worker drops to the ground after a particularly vicious blow, and the crowd boos as he shakes his head, trying to clear it. She shivers as the Walker stalks over and kicks him, her face unexpectedly pale. "Nurrin," I say, and her gaze snaps to me, revolted and pleading. "Eyes on me."

She nods, gritting her teeth, and I lead her through the crowd, punching a man when he throws a careless elbow that gets too close to Nurrin. We get caught in the melee of bettors exchanging money when the fight ends, and then we're near the wall. I find the only door and knock once.

A tiny Asian girl is sitting on the desk, a black man standing beside it. I eye them, and my fingers twitch, anxious for my gun. She shouldn't be here.

Finally, the little Asian looks up at me, a bored expression on her pale face. "What can the Blessed Order of the First do for you, Finn O'Malley?"

Chapter 5

The Day the World Stood Still

Everyone remembers the day the dead rose. Even those who had been small children can pinpoint where they were when the army hit the zombie horde outside of Atlanta. The world stopped, eyes trained on a five mile stretch between Atlanta and Newnan, watching while the entire fucking thing came crashing down around us.

I was with my parents—my father and his best friend sat side by side, watching on a tiny monitor as the horde from Atlanta slammed into the troops from Fort Benning and everything-—every fucking thing we'd ever known or would know—stopped.

The Blessed Order says it began on Day One. When Emilie Milan sat up and ate the morgue attendant. But I was there. I was watching. I listened to the frantic calls, the screams of the soldiers as the virus in their blood reacted to the horde. The screams changing to moans when they were infected and joined the horde they were sent to destroy.

I heard it all.

I've heard a thousand stories since that day. A girl who lost her virginity while the zombies stormed Atlanta. A trucker who shot his children rather than let them face this world, and then carried that weight for another six years. A woman who baked an apple pie and sobbed as she listened to a newscast—her son had been in the ranks that changed.

People had been in class, in church, in basement bomb shelters.

Collin had been in a hospital, sitting next to his parents and newborn sister.

My story isn't that different—I was with my family. I sat with the people who cared about me as the horde swarmed Atlanta and spread.

I played with my best friend under a desk when the dirty bombs hit Atlanta, obliterating the fifth largest city in the United States.

We were playing hide and seek when millions died from the nerve gas that did nothing against the zombies.

I was hiding in a corner while the world crashed down and the battle for the East Coast began.

Chapter 6

Negotiations with the Devil

I stare at the High Priestess of the Order, her black hair stick straight. A startling swatch of white hair hangs over one eye. I can feel the press of Nurrin at my back, her bristling energy and anger, but she's quiet. And the priestess doesn't know who she is—I've always been very careful to make sure they don't know who or *what* she is.

"I need medicine. My brother picked up a contact infection."

Her eye widens a little, but she doesn't respond except, "I don't know how that concerns me."

I let a cool smile turn my lips. People who survive a contact infection are rare, and the Order adores them—they hunt them almost as intently as they do Firsts. "Don't play coy, Lori. It doesn't suit you."

Anger sparkles in her eyes for a moment before it's locked down and she lifts a delicate shoulder in a shrug. "You won't give him to me. And I don't need more cured. I need a First. Can you give me one of those?"

I feel Ren's entire body pressed against my back. But she doesn't react at all. I keep my voice flat. "If you don't have your sacrifice, you won't find one this late in the season. Maybe you've finally killed them all."

She makes an irritated face and shakes her head. "No. We have our records. We know there are more—we just can't find them." Lori studies me. "Word from Haven 8's High Priest was that they had a First."

Nurrin's grip on my back tightens a little. I force a smile. "Then we're one step closer to the Blessed cure—everyone in Haven 8 was killed when it fell."

Her eyes go wide. "What are you talking about?"

She doesn't know—and it might be useful. "Information for medicine," I say. She makes an impatient noise, and I stand up, turning Nurrin.

"*Stop,*" Lori snaps, her voice a whiplash of fury. She hates being one-upped, which is what makes it so damn fun to annoy her.

"I don't have time for you to play games, Priestess. And you know I don't appreciate them."

She sniffs. "Fine. Tell me what you want."

"InsuSyntrix. Four three week courses."

"No information is worth that, O'Malley." Lori laughs.

I smile, lazy and confident. "Mine is. When you decide you're interested, you can find me."

The black man takes a half step forward, but Lori stops him with a single hand. Neither says anything to me as I escort Nurrin out of the tiny room. Another fight has started, and I drag her into the crowd, tugging her until her back is pressed against my front. She's stiff and furious, her breasts heaving under the material of her dress.

"We can't leave—Lori is watching, and it's safest if we enjoy the Underground before we make a departure."

"So we'll watch men pummel each other until Lori loses interest?" she hisses. It's the first thing she's said since we entered the Underground, and I'm pleased to hear how steady her voice is.

"Unless something else in the Underground captured your interest," I say. She inhales sharply, licking her lips.

My dick hardens, and there's nothing I can do to keep it from her, not with her pressed against me. I'm not willing to let her go.

"What the hell, Finn?" she whispers, furious.

"Chemical reaction, Ren. Nothing to worry about."

My words are dismissive, my tone condescending, but she twists, staring at me with curious, probing eyes. I see a question in them, but I don't have an answer, and if she keeps staring at me, her lips inches from mine, I'll kiss her and the consequences be damned.

"Eyes on the fight, little girl," I murmur. She smirks and looks back ahead.

I knew bringing her here was a risk. It wasn't my first choice, but last night was too dangerous—the Order had everyone on edge Day One. The Underground, when I watched it from the outside, was deserted. No one was near it—and going there when it was so quiet would reek of desperation.

I had thought my only concern would be walking a First into the Order's lair. But it's not—there's also the fact that I'm exposing her to something she's never seen.

If Dustin's done anything right as her friend, it's been keeping her away from the Order-run vice clubs.

We wait through two fights—one I bet on, and after collecting our winnings, I draw her tight against my body and lead her from the fight hall.

She stops near the kink club. There's a show happening—a girl is on the large wheel, two men behind her with floggers. Around them, the other club patrons are watching, lost in various states of sex and desire. I slide a glance at her, curious about her reaction.

Her eyes are wide and watching, her breath catching in her throat, so still she almost trembles. Her nipples are hard little peaks, pressing against the red silk of her dress. It hits me hard—she likes it. The kink club that leave so many with a sour taste in their mouth—she's intrigued.

For all that I've watched her for years, I didn't expect that. And it makes keeping my hands off her even harder.

"Come on, Ren," I say hoarsely. "Unless you'd like to join in, I think we've spent enough time here for the day."

A blush colors her cheeks, and she looks away. I wrap an arm around her and usher her out of the Underground.

Chapter 7

Bad Decisions

She trips along in her heels, and I bite back a sigh of irritation. Even knowing I'm the one who gave them to her doesn't make me any happier that we're still on the streets. Any other time, I'd have taken her out on my bike, but not in *that* damn dress.

"Finn," she starts, and I cut her a look, glaring in the bright street lights.

Rebellion fires in her eyes, but she doesn't continue. Not until we're in my little house, the door shut behind us, locks triple checked.

I let out the breath I seem to have been holding, tension easing out of my shoulders. It's like a weight has slipped off of them, and I can relax.

"O'Malley."

And just like that, it's back. I straighten, forcing myself to blankness, and turn to arch a brow at her. "What can I do for you, Nurrin?"

"I want some idea of what the hell we're doing," she says. "I need to know why the fuck you think taking me into an Order's lair—to their fucking Priestess—was such a bloody brilliant idea. If she had known, I'd be dead right now!"

I move without thinking, yet another bad decision in a night full of them. I shove into her personal space, and she takes a half step back. "Do you think I'd put you in danger? Do you think Collin would let you go with me if he thought I'd risk your life?" I demand.

"I don't think anything," she hisses. "I don't *know* anything—you won't tell me anything. You expect to march me into a death trap and then give me nothing. I want to know what the hell we're doing—Lori will make a demand. The Order does nothing for free, and the meds you're asking for—" She laughs, a sharp, disbelieving noise. "What are you willing to give her for that medicine? How high a price are Collin's and Dustin's lives going to carry?"

I make a disgusted noise and step away. It's either that or kiss her senseless. "Quit thinking so much, Nurrin. I won't risk your life—not as long as I need something from you. I'll do whatever Lori asks, because I won't risk Collin. Is that enough honesty for you?"

"No," she snaps.

I smirk. Turn away and walk into my room. "That's all you're going to get."

She stalks after me. "Tomorrow? What are we doing tomorrow? How long are we going to wait, Finn?"

My name on her lips is a curse and so damn sexy I can't stand it. I pull my shirt over my head and reach for my pants. Clearly, sex and nudity won't scare Ren away—but I'm too tired to give a fuck about this right now.

"Tomorrow, we'll wait for Lori to contact us. It's Third Day—lying low is our best bet, if we have to stay in the Haven."

She shudders, rubbing her arms. I want to do that for her, want to soothe away her fears. It's a bad idea, so I turn away and sit on the edge of my bed. "Just trust me," I say, quietly. "I won't put you in danger if I can help it. It'll just make my life more difficult. Get some sleep. I'll get what information that I can tomorrow—I want you inside, the door locked, until it's over."

She's pale and nods.

Even without a First, the Order will kill tomorrow. I just need to make sure it's not Ren.

Chapter 8

Third Day

I can hear her, the soft snoring she would never admit to making, through the thin walls. I lie on my bed, the silk sheets warm with my body heat against my skin.

It's the seventh of March. The day the world stopped. It began, twenty years ago, in blood. It ended in death and smoke, fire and ash.

I wish, sometimes, I could go back. Back to that corner where I stood with Kelsey, her fine blonde hair tickling my neck.

I shake my head, hard, dislodging the memory, and swing from my bed. Pad naked across the room and reach for my pants.

When I'm dressed, I slip from my bedroom. Hesitate briefly outside Nurrin's room. She snores quietly, and I grin. Not the calculated smirk that infuriates her, or the lazily manipulative one that seduces women to my bed—just a real smile. She wouldn't recognize me with this expression.

I whistle softly and go to the kitchen to make us breakfast. Not much—the house still gets rations because I demand it to maintain a home in the Haven and the aldermen want my presence—even my absent presence—here for the added protection.

Idiots. I can't offer them anything—Haven 8 falling showed that more eloquently than anything.

I peer out the window, checking the deserted streets. A small silver package is sitting on the walk up to my house. It's clearly placed for me to notice. I glance down the hall, to where her door is still closed.

God, I want the day over. Already, I'm anxious and impatient.

I put the coffee down and grab my knife. Holding it flipped with the blade flat against my lower arm, I slip out of the house and snatch up the package.

A member of the Order is standing in the middle of the road, masked face staring at me from the depths of its hood. I bare my teeth at it and retreat back into the house.

"Fucking creepy fuckers," I mutter, glaring at the closed door. I make a cup of black coffee and open the package.

Inside, there are two small vials of Kelaxon and a letter. I curse. This does nothing—it might slow the infection, if Collin has picked one up, but it's too late to do anything for Dustin.

Nurrin is going to be furious.

O'Malley,

A good faith gift. We will give you the antibiotics in exchange for information about the fall of Haven 8. And a retrieval of a package in Haven 21. Bring both to me in two days, and we'll make the exchange. This is the last time your name will carry any weight within our order, O'Malley. Make sure it's worth using.

HP-

I'm sitting there, holding the note in my hand and staring into nothing, when she finally stumbles, half awake, from her room. She mumbles something incoherent in my direction as she staggers to the coffee pot and pours herself a large cup. I wait for her to reach for the sugar, but she just leans against the counter and takes a large sip, black, her eyes closing in a blissful smile.

I look away, scowling into the note, and she shifts a little. "What's that?"

"The Order made their offer," I say. I drop the note on the counter and stand. "Be ready to leave in an hour. The sooner we're out of the Haven, the better."

I stalk to the front door—I need to pay Jesse a visit, get a vehicle. He should have something old school enough to get me through the wreckage and into the city.

"Lock the doors. Barricade yourself in the safe room—I'll get you out when I get back."

Her eyes are wide, all traces of sleep gone, replaced by anger. I don't have time for this. "Finn, you can't leave me!" she snaps.

"I can't take you this time. You know what those fucking lunatics are like on Third Day. I can't protect you—the best safety I can offer is that hole. Get your ass in it."

I slam the door behind me, punctuating my words, and lock it with my set of keys. She won't be able to leave, and if she locks herself into the zombie-proof safe room, she should be safe until I return.

Without letting myself consider that she won't be, I jog down the steps and break into a run.

It's a stupid move, but I'm too keyed up to care. The deserted streets work in my favor— Third Day is usually quiet until around three in the afternoon. I see a few cult members in their robes, but Lori must have passed word around— none of them approach me.

I hammer on Jesse's door for almost five minutes before he throws it open, cursing. I ignore his anger, shoving into the house. "I need a car. A Hummer or Jeep, if you have them. Fully stocked."

"When?" he asks, and I glance at him.

"Now."

He makes an amused noise in his throat. I frown, watching his expression slip from amused to *oh shit*. "Dammit, O'Malley, you can't keep pulling this shit."

"Actually," I drawl, letting my accent thicken, "I can."

He scowls, and I nod at the back of the house. "Do you have anything?"

"Not a fucking Hummer," he snarls. I want to punch him—the thought of his hands on Ren makes me violent, and his pissy attitude is just lighting the fuse on my temper.

"What do you have?" I demand, my voice low and controlled. Jesse's eyes narrow, and he strides toward the back of the house.

"An armored truck. Ford started production in Haven 46 last year. It's gonna cost a shit ton, though."

"Speed?"

"No gov. You can tap her out at 120—she's got a good sized tank, so you can easily travel between Havens. Where are you headed?"

I ignore the question and eye the truck. It's not my style—I prefer something a little sleeker or more obviously aggressive. But there's a gun turret mounted in the bed of the truck, which could be hella fun in a fight. I nod. "Make it happen."

"Dude—price."

I make an annoyed noise. "You know better. The money will be wired tonight. Keep the Porsche, too."

Annoyance flickers across his face, but I ignore it and head for the front door. "Get it to my place in thirty minutes. Fully stocked, Jesse."

"I didn't touch Ren."

I jerk around—and curse myself for reacting. Jesse's watching me, his eyes somewhere between amused and afraid. "I thought about it. I almost did—she's a hot little piece. But I wouldn't touch her."

I smile, coldly. "Thirty minutes," I repeat. And leave.

Chapter 9

A Changed World

Before ERI-Milan swept through the world, people lived in houses with porches, screen doors, and window that opened.

After the virus hit, things changed. Life went on—humans are too damn stubborn to quit completely—but it was different. America, Canada, Mexico—they were isolated from the European countries. Africa took longer to fall to the infection. All the third world countries fared better in those first few months than their more influential neighbors. They weren't dependent on ERI, so it didn't mutate in the population. But eventually, the tide of the dead hit them, and they didn't have a chance against the horde. Africa fell to the dead within six months, South America two months later. India and China were overwhelmed by sheer numbers, until the Chinese army rallied.

By then, we were alone, getting the barest of updates from the rest of the world. Fighting our own war against infection and trying to adapt—to survive.

It was an architect who created the bolt holes—a student at the University of Chicago, who hid in a basement vault in his apartment building until the dead finally took everything breathing and moved on. He was insane, a mess of crazy, when the National Guard found him a few days after the Fall of Chicago, but he had plans on him. A brick and metal safe, perfect for surviving.

He killed himself, two nights after the Guard bundled him onto a boat in the middle of Lake Michigan. Ate a bullet and scared the ever-loving shit out of the other refugees.

His plans lived on—now, every private residence is equipped with a Hale Hall. Over the years, they've been adapted and become big business in the northwest—not surprising since they originated there.

I approach mine, staring. It's top of the line—double steel walls, lined with zom repellent, coded to a body signature to open, followed by a retinal scan. It was the best money could buy, a neat little hole to waste away in. I press my thumb on the pad, and it warms, flashing green. The grip locks on me, and I feel the prick of a dart against my eye as the retinal scan activates—the dart is pressurized—if the scan picks up traces of the virus, it'll fire through my eye, lodge in my brain, and explode. Messy, but effective.

Even knowing I'm clean, I hold my breath as the light flashes an alarming orange then hits bright, blinding green. The grip on my head relaxes, and I lean back as the explosive dart retracts. There's a soft his of pressurized air, and the door swings outward. Ren is sitting cross-legged on the bench, her knee bouncing nervously. I force my smile down, away, and nod at the bag she's dragged in the Hale Hall. "What's that?"

"Clothes. Food—all the weapons I could find. Make sure I didn't forget something you want, and we're ready to leave."

A surge of pride and approval hits me, and I turn away, striding through the house and scanning it. There's nothing here—nothing that I give a damn about. It's just a place to rest and hide, a place where my past hasn't died completely.

I shouldn't have a past—not anymore. Everyone lost that when the zombies rose. I don't know why mine is the only one who seems convinced it's a zombie and won't just fucking die.

I crouch by a chair in the living room, prying the floorboard up and scooping out the cash and credentials I have hidden. I toss one travel pass to her. It's not her picture or her name, but the resemblance is close enough.

"Memorize that," I order, shoving everything in a bag and standing, kicking the floorboard back into place.

She's watching me, but doesn't say anything. I hear a roar on the road, and I grab her bag, tossing it over my shoulder as I lead her outside.

Her eyes are sparkling as she stares in fascination at the massive black truck, the thick bulky doors, studded with spikes. Razor wire wraps around the grill and tailgate—I could drive this through a horde and part them like butter.

Her voice is breathless and squeaky, hitting me straight in the groin, when she says, "Oh, Finn." I glance at her, and she grins at me. "Can I drive it?"

Chapter 10

War and Peace

She drives. When she asked like that, I could hardly deny her. And I could use the opportunity to go over the supplies she packed. The truck is fully outfitted with a field med kit and food, weapons and extra rounds of ammo for the machine gun.

"Is that really a gun on the truck?" she asks. Her voice, even an hour into our drive, vibrates with excitement. Good—I want her happy, not thinking about Third Day.

"Yup. Apparently, this is Ford's new model."

She whistles, petting it, and I feel an irrational jealousy for the steering wheel. "Must have cost a fortune."

Ren grins at me archly, and I laugh. "Quit fishing, Nurrin. I'm not answering shit."

She huffs a breath and stares broodily out the window.

"Why do you care so much?" I ask, keeping my voice deliberately neutral.

Ren snorts. "You're Collin's best friend, and I know nothing about you. You can afford neural inhibitors, and a top of the line tank, but you're a Walker and an orphan. You were somewhere you shouldn't have been when Hellspawn fell, but you saved my life. You hate me, but you kiss me."

Her words are so soft on the last one, I almost don't hear her. Almost.

"There's very little you need to know about me," I say, staring out at the passing mountains. The trees blur, flashing red occasionally as we speed pass infects. "My past doesn't matter. Money doesn't matter. The only thing that you need to know is that Collin trusts me and I won't put you in danger."

Her gaze darts to me, and I see questions brewing, the denial on the tip of her tongue. I turn to the back of the truck and slip through the little door that accesses the bed—and the machine gun.

I spend more time mentally retreating from her than I am comfortable with, but I'm not going to think about that right now. She hits the gas a little harder, and I slip on the steel bed, catching the gun and holding on as we race through the mountains and the desert, headed for the remains of Sin City.

Chapter 11

The End of Days

We hit Vegas at dusk, and I can hear the screams from the rubble outskirts. I slow to an idle and look at Nurrin. She's pale, her blonde hair sticking to her sweaty neck. "What's your name?" I ask sharply, and her gaze snaps to me.

"Kelsey Cain," she says. She rattles off a dead girl's birth date and statistics, and I nod approvingly. "You're Sean Jackson. Born in Buffalo, but moved west with the evac orders during the first wave. Mother and Father were killed when New York fell. Sister is alive and living in Haven 3."

I nod. "Good girl. Remember—nowhere without me. Not even a Hale Hall, do you understand? I have no presence in Vegas, and we're going without my name as backup, so we've got each other and nothing else. I'm going to get what we came for and get the fuck out."

She nods—Vegas is a hellhole at the best of times, and Third Day is a far cry from the best of times.

"Do you think it's already started?" she asks. I look out the windshield—smoke is rising from the ruined city, and the screams have increased in pitch, shrillness.

It's ironic, in the worst possible way, that The Blessed Order took Sin City as their headquarters.

"Yeah, Ren. It's already started," I say softly.

Her hand clenches and unclenches, and I push down the urge to reach for it, to smooth my thumb over her knuckles. She nods sharply, and I put the car in gear, easing us forward through the rubble.

Vegas—now Haven 21—is different from most Havens. It doesn't have walls, orchards, and fields. It doesn't have brick apartment buildings for the orphans and the forgotten. The streets aren't drenched in zom repellent.

Instead it has one single, shining monument to human depravity, a tower of sex and greed and stupidity. I pull through the wall of rubble, and Ren's fingers clench rhythmically on her gun. We drive through the streets without much fanfare or issue. The streets are clear of infects—startlingly so. But as we drive deeper into the city, closer to the Palace, the screams intensify, until they echo off the buildings, off the vehicles, off everything to bounce and reverberate. She huddles into herself, and I see the first one.

The infect is racing down the street, his face twisted in a gross distortion. One eye socket is empty, the other so decayed all I can see is blood. His hands are gone, splintery bones where the appendages should be.

He's grotesque, and I can't look away, even though I know what's coming. I see the sacrifice, running through the streets first.

The girl is young—not even a First. She's too young to be. Her eyes are wide, and she sees us, the truck, an instant before the zombie screams and jumps the last few feet. She stares, pleading, and then she screams, another voice joining the melody of wailing. I look away, jaw tight. Shove the truck a little faster. At my side, Ren makes a soft, distressed noise, and I cut my eyes at her. "She's gone, Nurrin."

Tears sparkle in her eyes, but she nods.

We pass three more token victims before we hit the main drag.

And then we stop, unable to move, and I'm suddenly grateful for the tank I paid a shit ton of money for. A zombie slams into Ren's door. She yelps, skidding across the bench until she's pressed against me, trembling as we stare at the decayed face and the gouges it's leaving on the glass.

"It's shatter proof, right?" she asks, breathlessly.

I nod, and she eases away from me. Drags her gaze from the zombie that's still battering at her window and onto the carnage.

It's a fucking bloodbath. The bodies are strewn across the Strip like trash, dead and dying. Clusters of zombies crouch over dead bodies, feasting on the bounty of the Order. At my side, Ren gags, and I grab a bag, shoving it at her as she heaves and throws up. It's disgusting and messy. It's what I would do, if I were a little less jaded. If I hadn't seen it for so many years.

Every Haven has their version of the Order— lesser chapters, small congregations. Most mid- sized chapters hold the Third Day Massacre. I want to say there's a method to their madness, but there isn't. There's only fucking insanity, a new, deadly kind in a world gone completely mad.

It began with Sawyer Russell. He'd been traveling with a group of survivors out of Chattanooga—everyone in the area was scrambling to get clear of the carnage spilling from Atlanta, and he landed on a hospital transport.

They had five Firsts—babies born the day Emilie Milan rose. Six more born on Day Two and Third Day.

Eleven in all. Eleven breathless, hungry, screaming babies.

The hospital transport hit a traffic snarl outside Cleveland, Tennessee, and they were left to walk. The first night, the screaming babies brought down a small pack—five zombies found the little house the group was hiding in. Sawyer was desperate, coming down off a wicked meth high. With the zombies literally at the door and a baby screaming, he did the only thing that made sense in his fucked-up mind. He tossed the kid out.

That nameless child was the first First. And when the zombies left, temporarily appeased, and his group beat the shit out of him and left him for dead, Sawyer was left to think.

He didn't die. Instead he rallied, and he found people desperate and degenerate. People willing to believe anything, any tiny lie that offered any kind of comfort.

When he said killing a First made the horde retreat, and killing them all would make the zombies die, people were desperate enough to believe him. Before anyone realized how dangerous he was, the Blessed Order was established—a dangerous, murderous group.

Sawyer took his insane followers and retreated to Vegas, raided the local army base, and turned what was left of a casino into a fortress.

All year, the casino is open. People can visit the gaming tables, the second-level clubs. The fight halls and races. On the upper floors, the strippers and prostitutes, the kink clubs.

And, in the basement, when everything is gone and you have nothing left, Sawyer and his cult of blood hungry bastards takes what little remains.

I wonder what that girl's parents had done— what they spent her lifeblood on. What vice kept them running in this pathetic excuse of a world?

The massacres are a tribute, Sawyer preaches. They're a tribute to the work that is done and being done, to God's judgment while we hesitate over killing the Firsts.

I think they're all power hungry lunatics, but I know better than to cross the Order in their seat of power. So I wrap my name up tight and drive us deeper into hell.

Nazarea Andrews

Part 3

The Future without Hope

*

The future belongs to those who prepare for it today.

Author Unknown

**

The future is uncertain—but we will fight for our way of life. Even as it changes.

President Andrew Buchman

Chapter 1

Casino Evil Incarnate

He says trust. He says nothing matters. He says he'll protect me.

He's fucking insane if he thinks I'm actually buying any of it. I thought this would be a quick trip—in and out, get the meds, drop the warning, and scoot back to the Hole and Dustin.

I didn't think we'd end up in the Order's stronghold on fucking Third Day.

The massacre is over. We inched down the Strip at a snail's pace for an hour or more. Then, like a switch had been flipped, the Order swarmed the streets in zom gear, picking them off with practiced precision. Within minutes, the zombie horde was slaughtered. Without acknowledging the truck we're sitting in, the Order stripped the dead of their weapons and retreated into the casino.

"We're going in there, aren't we?" I ask, forcing my voice to stay steady.

Finn nods, puts the truck in gear, and rolls over the dead toward the Casino.

They're waiting for us, guns bristling, and I shiver as he pulls into the parking garage and our truck is swarmed.

Finn shoots me a quick questioning look as the Order soldiers shout orders. I nod quickly, and he grins at me, shoving the door open. I slide across the seat. He tugs me down and wraps an arm around me, pulling me close as we face the Order.

"Name and Haven."

Finn grins, and his voice takes on a soft drawl. "Sean Jackson and my fiancée, Kelsey Cain."

I struggle to stand still and not react to that—it comes without warning.

"What's your business here?" the soldier demands.

Finn grins, a light expression that's out of place on his blank face. "What? I thought the Order liked visitors."

"it's Third Day, man. Not a day for visiting the vice clubs."

"Come on, dude. It took everything I had to save for this trip—and another two weeks of cajoling my girl's guardian. Don' tell me you're gonna refuse us entrance." There's an entitled whine in Finn's voice that makes the soldiers relax, a calculating gleam in their eyes.

"You have to pass an infection test." His gaze flicks to me, and a leer touches his lips. Finn's grip on me tightens minutely. The solider whistles sharply, and a gaunt-looking man in pale scrubs made bulky with armor hurries out with a test kit. The soldier's grip on his gun relaxes a little as the medic grabs my hand, jerking me out of Finn's grasp. He makes a low, angry noise, and I shoot him an annoyed look. The needle stabs into my finger, blood welling up. I hiss at the sting. The medic gives me an apologetic smile, then gives

Finn the same treatment. As soon as the vials settle into a deep red, the soldiers lower their guns and relax.

"Welcome, Sean and Kelsey, to the Keep of the Blessed Order."

Chapter 2

The Enemy's Gates

It takes another two hours to be sorted through the security and assigned a room. Finn pays the extravagant price with a remarkable amount of bitching, and finally, finally, we're escorted to the sixth floor, where our room is waiting. It's clean, done in white and gold, with sharp lines and one large bed. I stifle my sigh and Finn smirks.

As soon as the guard shuts the door behind us, he drops our bag and drags me into the tiny bathroom.

"What the hell are you doing?" I hiss as he presses me against the door and reaches to turn on the shower.

"The room is bugged. We can't act like anything but our cover stories—do you understand?"

He stares at me, and I remember what he said downstairs—I'm supposed to be his fiancée. I bare my teeth and snap, "You're fucking insane, you know that?"

The smile he flashes me holds more than a trace of crazy, and I think he knows it.

"Fine. What's the plan?"

"We need to get the eye of High Priest."

I shudder. I've spent most of my life avoiding that very thing. To be told now that I'm going to do the opposite—it's enough to make my blood go cold. Finn eases back, giving me space, and stares at me. "You can do this, Nurrin. Two days—less if we put on a good show tonight. We get what Lori wants and we go back to the Hole."

Back to Dustin and Collin—back with the medicine that *could* save their lives. I nod, and he gives me a rare, approving smile.

Two hours later, I'm really wishing I'd gotten more details before I agreed to this. I stare at the dress and shake my head. "No. I'm not wearing that."

Finn makes an impatient noise. "Quit whining and get ready—we're already late."

I give him a dirty look. He returned with the dress five minutes ago. I stare at it and then him and ask the question I've been avoiding, "Where are we going?"

Finn doesn't answer—surprise, surprise—but he does give me a dark smile before pushing me into the bathroom and closing the door.

I stare at the dress. I hate it, but my mouth waters a little. It's gorgeous, a fall of black silk and satin, flowers and spirals in jet beads, twisting up the side. It's got a high neckline and thin shoulder straps. The shocking part is the midriff, which is a sheer black material that rises in knife-like points. They rise up and around my breasts, drop low to brush my navel and hips. The back is completely sheer, dropping in a sharp point at the tip of my ass.

The dress is demure and daring, sexy as hell while keeping everything important tucked away.

Its eye catching and attention grabbing and everything I need to be tonight—in this dress all eyes will be on me. There's no way to float under the radar. The High Priest is sure to see us.

I heave a sigh and strip out of my clothes and underwear and shower quickly. I pull my hair up and apply my makeup. I use a light hand, making my lips almost a natural pink, and no blush. My eyes are dramatic, smudged and smoky, the blue jumping out. Then I dry my hair, leave a few curls hanging down, and pull the rest up. I add the peep toe heels and straighten, smoothing the wrinkles free and taking a deep breath. Then I open the door and step into the main part of our suite.

Finn is leaning against the side of the window, drinking something golden from a small glass. The sun is setting behind him, and for a heartbeat, framed by the opulent rooms and the sun, in a

black suit, black shirt, with a startling silver tie—
for a moment, he makes me freeze, emotions that
make no sense kicking around in my chest.

It's Finn. Finn O'Malley. The man who annoys
the shit out of me, who refuses to answer a simple
yes or no question, the one who made my brother
keep secrets from me.

The one who saved my life. Three times now.

I shove that thought down and take a half step
toward him. Of course he looks good. He's in a suit
and tie—even in blood stained-workout clothes,
Finn looks good. In a suit, looking out on the world
like he owns it and fuck the zombie apocalypse for
getting in his way? Then he looks positively edible.
It doesn't *mean* anything.

His gaze swings to me as he takes a sip of his
drink. I flush as he does a slow sweep over my
floor-length gown. His eyes are like a hot, physical
touch, sweeping me from head to foot and
lingering on all the interesting bits in between. I
clear my throat, and his gaze, sardonic and

amused, snaps to mine. "Do I meet with your approval?" I ask, cocking out a hip.

He shrugs and finishes his drink. Straightens his cuffs. When he looks back up, his gaze is cool and remote, as blank as he ever is. "You'll do. Let's go—we're late."

He leads me down the brightly lit stairways, and I try not to think of the last time I clattered down a stairwell with him, the alarms of Hellspawn chillingly quiet. He's holding my hand— part of the stupid façade—and I want to tug free and bolt the rest of the way down, until we're on level ground, with enough space to shoot anything that approaches.

Where memories don't echo off the tile and white walls.

His grip on my hand tightens, and it steadies me. Running would be weak. And if there is anyone I don't want to be weak in front of, it's Finn.

There's a third-floor restaurant, a place full of pristine tables and white tablecloths, beautiful women escorted by flawless men. He leans close and murmurs, "Follow my lead."

I slide Finn a look from under my eyebrows, but I don't respond as he steps slightly in front of me and speaks to the hostess. "Reservation for Sean Jackson and guest."

I bristle that all I am is a 'guest,' but the hostess smiles slightly and leads us to a small table, secluded to one side of the restaurant. She waits until Finn is situated comfortably next to me, and then smiles again. "The show will begin in a few minutes."

My mouth goes dry, and I lick my lips as she walks away. "What show?" I whisper.

"We're supposed to be in love."

"What show?"

"It's normal—a lot of newly engaged couples go to them. And looking like that, there's no way we'll slip under the radar. Especially not at this show."

My voice is shrill and a little hysterical. "What *show*, O'Malley?"

His gaze flashes hostile, and the lights in the room dim. I freeze as a server places two glasses of water on the table. He leans down and murmurs, "If you desire anything, I'm at your service."

I glance at him, startled to see the waiter is wearing only a few chains and a cup. Finn catches my gaze. I know he can see the shock there.

Then the stage comes into view, the silver pole. A girl is writhing on the stage to music that pounds in my blood like a spell. I lick my lips again, unable to look away.

The stripper teases for what seems like forever, long enough that I forget we're in a restaurant, surrounded by other patrons, long enough that I begin to forget that Finn is sitting beside me. She swings and sways, dancing, her head thrown back. And when she's finally naked, the man appears. He's naked, fully erect and carrying a pair of handcuffs.

I watch as she sinks to her knees and takes him in her mouth, her pretty blonde head bobbing while he keeps a hand tight in her hair. Until he finally pulls her away and secures her to the pole. Her breasts are high, nipples tight and shiny from his mouth. I think he'll fuck her—I almost want him to—but then he drops to his knees, hooks one of her legs over his shoulder, and licks. She screams, a noise of sheer pleasure, and I finally look away, overwhelmed.

I look straight into Finn's eyes.

Burning, hungry, and something else that flicks away so fast, I ignore it. He's watching me, and I can't breathe, can't look away as the girl's screams increase, as the noise from the crowd tells me she's not alone in her pleasure. She keens, and even then, he doesn't look away. A large, heavy hand cups the back of my neck, and he drags me forward, until our lips are a heartbeat away, the heat of his mouth almost scorching against mine. There's a moment of silence, and I lick my lips as the girl shrieks, the man groans. The tip of my tongue brushes against Finn's lips, and he growls, jerking me forward into his mouth and a bruising kiss. His hands are hard and hot on my shoulders, fingers rubbing over the material of my dress as I writhe closer to him in the tiny seat. He makes an impatient noise, nips at my lips, and I whimper.

I fucking *whimper*.

Distantly, I can hear the couple having sex on the stage, hear the slap of skin and the soft swell of breathing. But it's distant—so distant it could be another planet. Because for this heartbeat, this endless eternity, nothing matters but Finn, his lips on mine.

He sucks my lip into his mouth and bites down, hard enough that a lick of pain makes me jump. He shoves the table away from us. There's enough room for him to grab me by my arms and tug me into his lap. I settle against him, my legs on one side of his, my ass pressed against his erection— and need explodes through me. I thought it was there before, but feeling him hot and hard against my ass, teasing so close to where I'm aching for a touch—it drives me crazy. I grab his suit jacket and jerk him closer. He shoves his tongue in my mouth, all finesse and skill vanishing as lust slams into both of us. I feel like he's devouring me, his hand sliding down my shoulder to grip my breast.

I groan into his mouth at the touch, my entire body tight and achy for more. My nipple is pebbly and pushing into his palm. I want his mouth there. I pull away, a little, to tell him that, and his lips immediately find my throat, skating over my pulse point, teeth nibbling, and then he bites down, hard enough that I shriek, mindless of our surroundings and the girl screaming on the stage.

Nothing exists beyond right now—right this second.

I reach for him, between our bodies, and he bucks, an almost involuntary movement as I trace over the hard outline of his erection under his pants. I smirk and nibble at his earlobe.

"God, Nurrin," he whispers, harshly.

It's a bucket of ice cold water being dumped on my head. I jerk back, staring at him, and he goes still, waiting—watching me and gauging my reaction. His eyes are still hot and hungry, but his face is blank as he catches me around the waist, stopping me before I can scramble across the tiny booth and bolt. His lips are against my ear, but the passion is gone—his voice is icy cold and rough when he says, "Stay still—they're watching."

Relief floods me, and I almost sag into his arms—it was a show. A way to catch the Order's attention. Just like that kiss on the boat meant nothing, was just a way to make me take the neural inhibitors. This is the exact same thing.

"Are they coming?" I ask, and his gaze darts past me, searching the crowded room.

A grim smile turns his lips. "One more, Nurrin. Make it look real."

He kisses me again, before the warning settles, and I freeze as he plunders my mouth, sweeping in and exploring every crevice, rubbing over my tongue and flicking at my teeth, with just enough thrust and retreat that I can't help but think of sex. And thinking of sex with this man in my arms is dangerous—stupid in so many ways.

A soft noise jars my attention, and I peer up. I know how I look as I stare blankly at the waiter—my gaze sleepy and sexed-up, my lips swollen from kisses, my dress and hair in disarray.

I look freshly fucked, and I know it. The gleam of appreciation in the waiter's eyes makes me want to preen. "The Priest would like to invite you to his private rooms, sir."

"Thanks, but we're happy here," Finn says, drawing me closer.

The waiter makes a slightly pained face, and I smile, slip out of Finn's lap. "Come on, babe."

Finn frowns, but lets me tug him out of the booth. The waiter beams, a slightly idiotic expression, and turns to lead us through the club. The other patrons are lost in their own private worlds, watching, or fucking, or being watched while they fuck. I ignore them as I let Finn guide me through the room, now reeking of sex, and into the hall.

Chapter 3

Tangled Webs

The waiter leads us to a bank of elevators and keys in a quick code before offering us a final smile and retreating back down the hall to the pounding music of the dinner show. I shiver as the elevator doors swoosh closed, and at my side, Finn is tense and waiting. His arm is wrapped loosely around my waist, but his attention is turned away, and I'm glad. I need the break, however brief.

Being constantly under Finn O'Malley's scrutiny is exhausting work. We glide up into silence, and I stare out the window at the darkness of the ruined desert city.

"Have they killed her yet?" I ask, and Finn's gaze darts to me. He hesitates—Finn. He never hesitates.

"No. Not yet. Soon, though."

I shiver, and the elevator slows. With a deep sigh, Finn gathers me close, fixing an appropriately cocky and disdainful expression on his face. I stare, fascinated by the change, and he pulls me tight to him, my entire body pressed to his side as the elevator stops and the doors open.

The night sprawls before us—twinkling stars and darkness as far as I can see. On the very edge of the horizon, the sun is teasing still, a deep twilight cloaking the edge of the world.

A light brightens when we step into the room. It takes a heartbeat or two to realize we're in an apartment—the kind of apartment I've never seen, but still.

"It's the penthouse," Finn murmurs, surveying the wide area. It's clean and sparse, the décor and furniture clearly expensive.

The room appears empty, but there's a charge to the air that makes me nervous. I shift closer to Finn, instinctively twisting to give him my back as I sweep the room.

And that's how I see the priest first. He's in black robes, a shadowy figure in the dark room. His head is bare, the cowl pushed down. And he's watching us, an amused, calculating gleam in his black eyes. I squeeze Finn's arm, and he twists, staring at the priest.

And curses.

I jerk, startled, away from Finn. There is anger and annoyance in his face, and a recognition that makes me sick. What did I just walk into? What did Finn walk me into?

"I didn't expect to find you so far west, O'Malley," the black priest says, stepping away from the wall.

Why does everyone say his name with such familiarity? Is there anyone who *doesn't* know this man? How did I ever think he was just an orphan Walker?

"You underestimate me, Omar. Always have," Finn says easily.

Omar shrugs. "it's easy to underestimate what you don't see. It's been a while since you were in Haven 1."

Finn's gaze hardens. "Why are you here? And in those robes?"

"I joined the Blessed Order when we lost the Virginian border," Omar says. I blink—that was almost ten years ago, one of the last major defeats in the Battle for the East. Has it really been that long since he's seen this man? And if it has, how does Omar still remember Finn?

"I never took you to be a religious man, Omar."

"I never thought we would concede the East." There is a hint of accusation in Omar's voice that makes no sense.

Finn's eyes go frosty, and he says, quietly, "Wait for me in the other room."

"No," I answer, and he twists to glare at me. "You can't just kick me out of the room whenever someone brings up something you don't want me to know.

Finn's expression tightens, and Omar laughs, the noise odd coming from a giant priest. "She's feisty. As spirited as Kelsey was."

"Don't," he snaps, and the word is harsh, savage. A knowing gleam flicks in Omar's eyes, but I'm hung up on the name—the same name I'm supposed to be using here. "Who is Kelsey?" I ask, my voice shaking.

Omar doesn't answer. Whatever issues are between the two, he won't give me information.

"Shouldn't you be at the sacrifice?" Finn says, and Omar shrugs. "I would think the High Priest would want to be there for the miracle."

"The miracle is nothing more than mindless beasts following their limited nature. Finn O'Malley arriving in my casino with a lovely Kelsey lookalike in tow—that's something else entirely. Why are you here?"

"I'm running an errand for Priestess Lori."

Omar frowns. "What does she want?"

"It's your Order, man. You tell me why I'm here."

Omar's eyes skate to me. "Perhaps it'd be best if we discussed alone."

Finn's shoulders relax. I glare. "You're both shutting me out? Good to know the Order and you have something in common."

Finn doesn't respond. Omar eyes us, as if he's trying to decide what the dynamic is and what to say—but he's made it clear he stands with Finn.

"I'll have her escorted back to your suite."

"Don't bother," I snap, stalking to the elevator. I can feel Finn's gaze following me, and as I turn in the empty elevator to stare daggers at him, he takes a half step toward me. For the first time, I see indecision on his normally blank face. Then the doors slide shut, and I'm left on my own, without answers. Again.

Chapter 4

Searching for Truths

I'm supposed to go to our room—I know that's where he wants me. And I swore to go nowhere without him. But fuck Finn and his demands and vague promises, his refusal to answer questions and his kisses—especially his kisses. Fuck it all.

Without letting myself think through the wisdom of it, I stab the ground level button, and the elevator glides into motion.

As I descend, I think about the conversation that just took place. Omar knew him. From before the fall of the East.

When the zombies rose, there were some places that fared worse than others—Atlanta fell first, in a wave of dead and the ash of bombs. New York City and Boston, Pittsburg and Philly all fell quickly—the infection hit hard and spread fast in the urban environments, and no one knew how to combat the rampant spread of it. There weren't enough weapons to make a dent in the cities.

The United States government evacuated DC first—moved them all to Haven 1, a fortress-like max security prison in Idaho. Over the first two years, they evacuated as many as they could, building Havens as quickly as possible, with what was left of the Army defending the construction. When the civilians were as safe as the government could make them, attention turned back to the northeast—and the battle that would become a war, a war that would last for ten years, began. Every time we gained ground, the zombies would push us back. We'd kill a horde in Pittsburg, and a week later, another would dart in, driven by hunger and drawn by the stench of death.

I'd heard of wartime converts—the military who fought and lost the East when we eventually waved the white flag and retreated to the safe zone.

Not that it was—not really. Even the safe zone had the Wide Open, and that was undisputedly the zombies' land. We only traveled through it, and all of us were living on borrowed time.

The Order thrived when we lost the East. They grabbed the military up faster than anyone could believe. Before the East was declared unrecoverable, the Order was just a fringe group that was annoying and a little dangerous. But with the backing of so many military, they became something else—something everyone was afraid of.

By then it was too late. The Havens were fractured, the government was in shambles, and when the Order retreated into what was left of Vegas, everyone breathed a collective sigh of relief.

The elevator dings pleasantly, and the doors slide open on a spacious, quiet hall. I can hear the soft murmur of the gaming room, and I turn toward it. I have no real interest in the games, but maybe I can find a drink—getting drunk seems like a brilliant idea, suddenly.

After the dinner club and what I saw in Haven 18, I'm not sure what to expect from the Order's casino. I've seen films of them before the change, when they were brightly lit and filled with glittering people playing at velvet-lined tables and sitting in front of rows of slot machines, drinking and smoking and winning.

It's nothing like that. A few guards in Order robes patrol the edges of the massive room, and tired looking men and women loiter around dirty, scratched tables, piles of chips in front of them as blank faced dealers pass out cards and collect money. A waitress, wearing a sedate uniform instead of the chains and strategically placed cups, pauses near my arms. "Are you wanting to play, miss?"

I look at her, at the startled respect in her eyes. I don't fit in here—not wearing this dress that Finn put me in. I can feel the spark of interest from the men at the tables, the disdain from the women watching their men. I am distantly aware of the attention of the guards and the realization that this might not have been my most intelligent move ever.

The waitress is still waiting, a hopeful look on her face. "No," I say, shortly. I'm not here to gamble away what little I have—the Order is dangerous enough to me without lining their pockets and selling my freedom. "I only want a drink."

A small smile turns her lips and she motions. I follow her deeper into the casino, aware of the eyes chasing me and the soft murmur of conversation that swells behind me as I make my way to the bar. It's a pitted, pockmarked thing of oak, rounded and smooth from hands rubbing against it, and time. I rest my arms lightly, and the bartender, a boy who looks younger than me by a year or so, approaches. His eyes are tired, but his smile is bright. "What can I get you, lovely lady?"

"A beer," I say. He nods and turns to the tap, and I wonder why I didn't just keep my mouth shut. I don't want a beer—I don't even *like* beer. And there is the small matter of this dress still.

"Do you know where a girl could get a little privacy and quiet?" I ask as the bartender places the beer carefully in front of me.

"How much privacy?" he asks, seriously.

I motion to my dress. "Somewhere I won't be stared at."

He hesitates for a long moment, and I give him my most beseeching eyes. Finally, he cracks the barest of smiles. "Come on then—I don't want you to be stared at either. The girls don't like it when something competes for their tips."

I give him a hostile smile and he takes a half step back.

"Sorry, miss." His head drops, respectfully, as he comes around the oak bar and leads me past the edges of the casino. The deeper in we go, the odder the games become—a cat chases a mouse in one cage. I stop, half appalled when it catches it's victim and rips into it. The watchers cheer, and a few fistfuls of chips change hands. But most are still, waiting, as the cat paces its cage, yowling and hissing.

"What are they waiting for?" I ask, and the bartender glances over. Something flickers across his gaze before he looks away.

"The change." He says shortly, striding away. I glance back, my stomach twisting as I realize the mouse had been infected. The cat is slowing, stumbling. As I stare, it screams, falling over.

The mouse had been dosed with ERI-Milan, heavily—there's no way the cat could change that fast without something to instigate it. I shudder and hurry after the bartender, almost tripping over my heels in the process. "Why?" I ask, my voice low.

He glances at me and shrugs. "Blood sport is a paying game, miss. And the Order needs money to run."

I don't respond. For a moment, I had managed to forget where I was—the beast whose belly I traipsed through. Now, I can't help but think of it, and I feel a slither of cold fear—maybe this is a bad idea. Maybe going back to the room is the best idea I've had all night.

"In here, miss."

I look up, startled out of my thoughts, and gasp as he leads me into a large ballroom. It had to have been an events room, before the change—it's wide, with high, heavy walls and a vaulted ceiling soaring above us. My heels clack on the marble as I step inside, staring around.

It's a massive library. The walls are lined with books, tables ordered nearly with stacks of newspaper clippings.

There's always been rumors about the Order. Rumors they are in the slave trade, that they buy children and raise them to be killers, rumors that they experiment in the depths of their compounds, looking for a cure to the disease everyone knows can't be cured.

And there is talk of a library, a vast collection of clippings, newspaper articles from the change that are gathered and collected—here, apparently.

A soft light glows through the room. I want to look through the record of the Change.

"Will this be quiet enough, miss?" The bartender asks.

I turn, smiling at him. "It's perfect, thank you so much."

He nods and starts to turn away. "Oh. You are, of course, welcome to pursue our shelves. Make yourself at home."

My fingers twitch, involuntarily, at his words. I wait as he smiles one last time and slips out the door. In the sudden quiet, I take a deep breath, inhaling the scent of mourning incense and smoke, leather and hot plastic. I take a step toward the bookshelves and pause. Omar's words from upstairs are still echoing in my head. He seems to ascribe to the same philosophy on information as Finn—which means virtually none. But after a little time with him, I'm getting better at picking up Finnformation. He gave me more than he thought—more than he probably wanted. I grab a few books at random and sit at the table stacked with papers. They're neatly ordered, divided by Haven and month. I grab a stack about Haven 1 and start paging through it. There's almost no chance that a random child would have been documented during the change—the only one who mattered was Emilie Milan, and after her death triggered the change, no one was able to spend much time reporting any news. Not until things settled, and that took almost two years.

But there was always news from Haven 1. It's where the government retreated to—the president and his advisors sent out news bulletins to keep people's hope up.

There wasn't much beyond that—emergency PSA announcements, a few articles about the measure to approve Haven building and mandatory evacs.

One name—Sean Finnegan—keeps popping up. A friend of the President Buchman. He worked with WHO and led the CDC team trying to find a way to combat the infection. I see him again and again, until the fall of Detroit three years after the change. I don't remember that—but Collin does.

Detroit fell in a wave of blood. No one expected it. The cold slowed the infects, and the gun-toting gangs put them down almost as fast as the zoms rose. Then a horde swarmed—one that migrated down from Canada, and the city collapsed under the sheer numbers of the zombies.

The scientist is briefly mentioned—a tragic casualty in the fall. The president hosted a funeral, which raised a few eyebrows and made the news, such as it was. There was a blonde girl there, a pretty, thin creature standing, somber and dignified, next to the president and the casket.

The president's daughter.

I dig back, pondering the information I have. Finn has a slight accent, which means he originated somewhere else—and was probably trapped here by the zombie apocalypse. He has contacts everywhere and enough money to move small mountains.

And the High Priest of the Blessed Order knows him from a past life. That is the hardest part to reconcile, the part that doesn't fit. Who was he—who were his parents—when the world ended? It's the only way to explain his wealth and prestige.

I flip the file closed and reach for the stack that's largest—the articles that follow the Battle for the East.

There was a small contingent of college students who couldn't put aside their civil rights hang-ups and refused to fight the zombies. Most of those were eaten. The only civil right a zombie cares about is the right to eat anyone's brain.

The only use for people like that was reporting, and in that crazy time, everyone needed to have a use. So they were sent to the front lines, reporting back during the war. A lot of them died. Those who didn't got over their civil rights issues and killed, because that is the only way to survive in this world.

I find Omar in the eighth article. There's a square box of text detailing an offensive to reclaim

Methuen, a small town in Massachusetts. Omar is mentioned in the article, but it's the picture that captures my attention.

Omar was young—younger than I am now. But he was still a small mountain of a man, his body wrapped in fatigues and zombie-resistant armor. His expression is lighter somehow, more hopeful.

Before the inevitability of the war hit him.

There are other people in the picture, but the one who draws my attention stands at Omar's right, a blank expression on his face.

He looks the same. Same empty eyes, lithe body, close-cropped hair. Same full lips that refuse to smile. Same disdainful impatience oozing from his negligent disregard of the world around him.

Finn. He fought in the war—they *let* him. It doesn't explain his wealth, but other things make a little more sense, the foggy lens of who he is twisting into focus a little more.

I hear him enter the room, the air charged with his irritation as he stalks toward me.

I slide the article away and twist in my chair to meet him. Sitting feels too vulnerable, standing too aggressive. There is no good way to confront Finn O'Malley.

He stares at me in silence for a few moments, long enough that I want to fidget, but refuse to.

"What are you doing, Nurrin?" he asks, finally, his voice low and tightly controlled. Even with that control, he sounds furious, and it makes my own anger swell to meet his.

"Reading," I answer blandly.

"You're fishing," he says, glancing at the closed files in front of me.

"Does that bother you? I don't believe in blind trust, O'Malley, and you've done nothing to earn mine."

His expression tightens—something about that bothers him. But he doesn't address it, doesn't tell me why. Instead, "I told you nowhere alone."

Really? "That's your hang up?" I demand, my voice going up a little despite my effort to remain calm. "You kicked me out, remember? You didn't want me overhearing whatever was so damn important. Well, fuck you—you can't decide that and then expect me to trot back to the room like a docile little wind-up toy. I'm not that girl, and I'm not your arm candy. If that's what you want, pretty sure there's a whole casino full of girls who can keep their mouths shut. Go find one," I snap.

"You have no idea what you're talking about," he says tightly. "And being angry isn't an excuse for risking your life, you fucking idiot."

I smile, a nasty edge to it. "You have to give a damn to be angry."

I finally stand, and Finn is close enough that I can feel the heat if him a hair's breath away, a slip of air and cloth separating us.

"If you risk yourself again, because you're too fucking impulsive and childish, I'll chain you to the damn bed until its time to go home."

I blink, almost take a step back. He's got that look in his eyes, the one that is feral and disturbing.

"Do you understand me?"

"If you touch me, I'll cut your balls off and feed them to you," I whisper.

He smirks at me. "Last time I touched you, you liked it, little girl."

Rage and humiliation flare through me, chasing a spike of arousal. "Go fuck yourself," I snap.

He shoves me into the wall, his mouth hovering above mine, and I can almost taste him. I push back against the wall, as far from him as possible. "Collin will kill you for this," I whisper, and I hate that my voice shakes.

Regret flickers over his face, briefly, and he steps back, giving me a little breathing room. "You might be right about that. But I would risk it to have you alive."

"Why?" I ask, before I can stop myself.

He steps away, and I can breathe, the air slipping through me and leaving me weak in the knees.

"Come on. Omar invited us to dinner."

Chapter 5

Invitations

The room we go to isn't a public one. It's quiet, hidden from the crowds. Here, there is no noise from the casino, no mourning incense, none of the lightly clad waitress and heavily armed guards. Here there is only a table, low hanging lights, and the mountainous black priest. He watches us with curious detachment as Finn escorts me across the room and waits for me to sit. The table is already set with plates of chicken in a creamy sauce and lumpy potatoes, a salad topped with vinegar and oil, and a crusty loaf of bread. I stare at the wine as Finn drops with negligent grace next to me.

"Eat," Omar says, waving at the food. I reach for the wine, and Finn calmly reaches out, slapping my hand down. He stares at his friend in silence. Omar makes a half smile, half grimace. He takes a healthy sip of my wine and a small bite of everything on my plate. Finn doesn't say anything, just watches him for a long time before some of the tension eases out of him and he nods at me. Omar shakes his head, a little. "A lesser man would find your suspicions offensive, my friend."

"A lesser man wouldn't find me at the table with him," Finn answers. He doesn't reach for food, but I'm starving, so I take a mutinous bite. Screw him and his suspicious ass.

"What do you want, Omar?" I ask. He's already spoken to Finn—anything that was important, anyway. I'm under no delusions about my importance to this man.

"It's Third Day," he says simply.

Shit. Finn goes tense and alert next to me, and I shift in my seat, an instinct as old as I am raising its head. I want to bolt, find a hole to hide in until the danger has passed. Finn's fingertips brush my leg, and I shiver, but stay in my seat. The two bites of chicken roll nervously in my stomach, threaten to make a reappearance. This is why he wasn't eating.

"The sacrifice is in a few minutes. I wanted to extend an invitation to join us."

For a heartbeat, I don't understand him. He can't have offered that. No one but the Order observes the sacrifice—it's one of their most closely guarded rituals.

"We wouldn't want to intrude," Finn says, tensing to stand.

Omar smiles, a wolfish expression, all teeth and menace. "I insist."

Finn slides a glance at me, a question in his eyes. I force a sick smile. Finn looks back to Omar. "Lead the way, friend."

Chapter 6

The Stuff of Nightmares

The casino has been emptied, and above us, there is a low, long wail of a siren. I freeze, and Finn's arm wraps around my waist like a steel band, pulling me close and dragging me along.

"What is the story, here?" Omar says, glancing over us. "I know her name can't really be Kelsey."

"She isn't important to you," Finn says, and his voice is so dismissive tears actually sting my eyes. I stare at the floor, ignoring both of them as I stumble after the two men through the deserted casino. Omar's gaze rests on me, a hot brand of pity.

What would he do, if he knew that Finn hadn't brought a piece of ass into his stronghold, but a First?

Stupid question—he'd throw me into a cage until next year's sacrifice.

We reach the back of the casino, and Omar presses a code into a small box by a vault door. A tiny blood test appears, and he waits while the needle pricks his finger. It flashes green and the door slides open. Three armed guards are waiting on the other side, guns pointed at us.

"Stand down." Omar barks the order sounding more like a drill instructor than a priest, and the soldiers snap to obey. One hesitates, and Omar steps into his space, the gun barrel pressing against his chest. The soldier's eyes go wide and startled. "Stand. Down," Omar murmurs, his voice like a roll of thunder.

It makes sense, now. How a decorated war hero became the High Priest in the Stronghold. A militant order needs a militant leader.

"They are my guests," Omar says. The soldiers glance over us curiously as Omar leads us past them, into a long narrow hallway. With each step, I can hear the beat of drums and the chanting of the Order—the sacrifice is near, and the faithful have worked themselves into a frenzy that this will be the time, the last First that needs to die to end it all.

If there is anything that makes me think humanity should have died when the zombies rose, it is the idiotic blind faith of the Order. We're too stubborn for that though.

As we round a corner, the noise of the crowd swells to a fever pitch, a hysterical beating of drums and shrieks for salvation. I stare at the arena. Before the change, it was a place for entertainment, a place to watch men box and women in tiny outfits parade around them. It was a place of depraved amusement—and now, it's a floor stained with the blood of my sisters and brothers.

The boxing ring has been modified a little—chain link fencing, fortified by steel bands, circles it, topped with razor wire. It's what we use to protect our schools and children in a Haven, what tops our walls—the wire is perfect for catching and shredding anything that comes near it.

And now it will trap the sacrifice.

Omar steps into the room, and a acolyte in a scarlet robe immediately moves to stand next to him. "Trina will take you to your seats. We'll talk again, after the sacrifice."

Finn watches Omar as he strides into the mass of Order faithful. The robed sea parts before the black priest, his black robe licking at the people he passes.

Our seats are in the front, a small, secure box. We're separated from the masses, a position of some importance. And one where we can't avoid what's happening.

"Can you watch this?" Finn asks, his voice warm in my ear. I nod, jerkily.

Omar's voice booms out, over the drums and chanting, "Faithful! Bring forth the sacrifice!"

The chanting falters, and a shrill scream rips through the room, hitting the spectators like fuel to a fire. They surge, a physical wave of people, desperate to reach the girl being ripped from her little hidden room. The scream comes again, chasing chill bumps over my skin. I know that noise. It's broken and shrill, furious and hungry. It's the noise of mindless desire and death.

People thought, before the change, that zombies moaned. They don't. A moan is the noise someone makes when they are dying, when they are broken. Zombies scream—because only a scream can convey the rage they feel, and the endless hunger.

I clench my eyes closed, and distantly, I'm aware of Finn prying my hand off the chair, wrapping my fingers around his own, a calloused anchor holding me in the here and now, reminding me he's given me a promise.

The girl comes into view, and I struggle not to flinch. Her hair is long and blonde, braided neatly. Her green eyes are wide and unseeing—she's drugged out of her mind. It's a small blessing. Her handler shoves her into the cage, and she blinks against the blinding lights, a hand coming up to shield her eyes. Her dress is simple, a white flowing garment that covers her from throat to toe. She's perfect—a pure, untouched First.

"As we were saved the third day by a First, may we be saved again. And may the blood of the Firsts appease the Unclean—may it earn their grace and our salvation."

"Grace and salvation," the faithful chant back, almost orgasmic in their fervor.

Omar closes his eyes, and Finn's grip on my hand tightens. Her eyes, blank and unseeing, meet mine, a tiny half smile on her lips.

And the chute opens, a pack of five zombies tumbling down from the ceiling to land in the ring. One lands wrong, and the snap of its leg reverberates through the sudden silence of the crowd. I bite down hard on my lip, desperate to keep my scream inside as the zombies survey the room. One, a big male with a bloody chest wound and blood-clotted eyes, sniffs and throws his head back, screaming.

It breaks through the drug haze, and behind the zombies, the girl whimpers. A female whips around, her teeth bared as she hisses and sees the girl. It takes less than two seconds for the other four to locate her, and less than three for the girl to realize she's fucked.

She screams as the first zombie lunges, rolling away. Black gore and blood from the zom smears on her dress, and she stumbles as the infect catches a better hold, jerking her closer. I'm surprised when she lashes out, kicking the zombie squarely in the face. He stumbles, a screeching whine building in his throat. The girl uses the second of time she's bought to jump on the fence. Below her the zombies are battering it as she climbs, shaking the links and jumping for her scrambling feet. Two have turned away and are snapping at the fence, fingers stretched to reach the crowd on the other side. There's a murmur of discontent from the crowd. I have a heartbeat of thinking she'll get away, that she'll find her way to safety.

Then she hits the razor wire, and the scent of blood hits the zombies. The girl screams as the zombies converge under her, shaking the fence and lunging upward at her, driven mad by the scent of blood and flesh. She shrieks as two infects slam into the fence, making it buck and almost throwing her off. She clutches at the razor wire, and I can see it digging into her fingers, slicing through them. Her eyes squeeze shut, and she screams, an agonized noise, as the sheer bladed metal bites deep, deeper. A finger falls into the pack of zombies, and Finn mutters a curse next to me. I'm barely aware. Her eyes have opened again, her pretty face contorted by pain and fury. Her eyes lock on mine again, and I flinch, almost look away.

And then she falls and the only thing I can see is a spray of blood. The wet sound of her scream, and ripping flesh, the sound of broken teeth eating. I can't—I look away, bury my head in Finn's shoulder and try to hear anything but this— anything but the screams of approval now coming from the Order and the sound of zombies tearing apart a girl whose only sin was being born the day the world went to hell.

Chapter 7

In Memorial

I keep it together until Finn shuts and locks our door. Then I drop to my knees on the too-soft carpet, a wail building in my throat. It's been building and demanding release for hours—since the First was killed, her screams silenced by hungry infects. Through the slaughter that followed, when snipers put the zombies down as priests swayed behind the distracted creatures. After, while Finn spoke to the black priest and I stood there like a pretty doll. I kept it together through all of it, because falling apart in front of the Order wasn't an option.

But here, with no one but Finn to witness it? I hit my knees with bruising force, my dress digging into my skin. He crouches next to me, extending a pillow silently. I snatch it from him and scream, my voice muffled by the lumpy pillow. I can feel Finn moving around the room, but I'm lost in my own thoughts, private agony, and the disgusting feeling that's ripping through me. My stomach twists, and I gag. The pillow is ripped away and a small trash can appears before me a second before I lose it, heaving into the little bucket. My sides ache, muscles clenching as I gag.

Finally, I slump on the ground. A wet rag lands in front of me, and I look up, faintly amused that Finn is taking this much care of me. He's loosened his tie and unbuttoned the top two buttons of his shirt. A sliver of skin glows alabaster in the dim light of the room.

I swallow hard as he stares at me, and for the first time all night, I remember the little strip club we started in tonight, and his lips on me. The untamed hunger in his eyes when he stared at me. There's nothing to buffer me from that now, and that is almost as disturbing as the sacrifice was.

"I can see you thinking," he says, and I shrug. There's nothing to really say to that. "What did you learn in the library?" he asks.

Ah. This. Damage control—how much did I learn and what kind of spin can he put on it? "It doesn't matter," I say, standing. "Unzip me."

Something flickers across his face, but he doesn't say anything. Stands behind me and slowly drags the invisible side zipper down. Heat from his fingers brushes against my skin, but he doesn't linger or go anywhere inappropriate. And when the zipper is completely down, my dress open and revealing me from the curve of my hip to the swell of my breast to the top of my armpit, he steps away.

I retreat to the bathroom and change into Collin's old workout shirt and a ratty pair of shorts. Finn is staring out at the silent, dark city when I emerge, backlit by nothing but blackness this time. I feel, vaguely, a sense of deja vu.

"It was never this dark, before," he says, softly. Almost speaking to himself.

"Did you come here?"

His gaze flicks to me, and he makes a face. "No. Come on, get in bed. You've had a long day."

I don't argue. He's right, and I'm exhausted—all I want is to close my eyes and let today disappear completely. I climb onto the massive bed and settle on my side, sinking into the plush comfort, the pillow almost swallowing my head. I tug the blankets up and around me and close my eyes. A few minutes later, there is a dip in the weight of the bed as Finn lies down then jerks the covers a little. I pull back and mutter, "Cover hog."

I must already be asleep. I know I must be dreaming his laugh and soft, "G'night, Ren."

Chapter 8

The Order's Agenda

I sleep hard, straight through the night. There aren't any dreams—or if there are, I forget them in my exhaustion. That I am sharing a bed with Finn doesn't even bother me. I'm too tired for anything to bother me.

A fist pounding on our door jerks me, rudely, into waking. I stifle a shriek when I see Finn, crossbow loaded and pointed at the door. The blanket shifts, pooling around his waist, and I flash back to him, standing naked and wet in the shower, him tackling me.

God, my first priority really needs to be getting laid, because this is getting ridiculous.

The pounding comes again, and then the deep voice of Omar, snapping at his men for disturbing us. I expect Finn to relax at the sound of his friend, but if anything, he seems more agitated, his body stiff, muscles vibrating with tension. I stare at him in confusion, and ask the first thing that I can think of, "How on earth did you smuggle that into the Stronghold?"

Finn's gaze skates to me, amused and disbelieving and, I shrug. A simple girl requires simple answers when shit get complicated.

"Finn. I need to speak to you, old friend," Omar calls through the thick door. Finn doesn't respond, and I roll out of bed. The door opens before I can reach it, Omar stepping in and shutting the door in the face of his soldiers.

Omar's gaze slips over me, taking in my clothes—and lack thereof—before slipping past me to Finn. He's still sitting in our bed, naked from the waist up, crossbow at the ready.

"Put that down, idiot," Omar grumbles, sidling past me without touching me. "Get up. We need to talk."

"It couldn't wait until I'd gotten a shower?" Finn asks, letting the crossbow drop into his lap. I notice his finger is still on the trigger. So does Omar, whose lips twitch in amusement.

"Are you planning on killing me in the Stronghold? Do you think you could escape if you did?"

"I've gotten out of worse," Finn says, not bothering to deny the wild accusation. Omar laughs at that, grinning, the first unguarded expression I've seen from him.

"You really think you could—and I'm half inclined to believe your claim. You got us out of Cinncy."

Finn's face is blank as he swings his legs down and stands. "Tell me what you want."

"What is Lori offering you?"

Finn pauses, his eyebrows going up. "Meds."

"Bullshit. There's no med you need that you can't get your hands on," Omar shoots back, and I twist to stare at Finn. "That's why we kept you around—why we needed you so damn much."

"That was a long time ago, Omar. Things change."

"Not that."

Finn's lips thin, and they both fall silent, staring at each other. I can't stand the tension thickening in the room and burst out, "Is that true? Can you get the meds to save Dustin?"

Omar startles, visibly, and Finn curses. "Shut *up*, Kelsey."

I hate that name on his lips, hate him calling me anything but my name. Hate that it belonged to someone I know nothing about. "Tell me if it's true, O'Malley."

"No. Dammit, no. I can't get anything without bartering. I haven't been able to for years. Which I just fucking told Omar, or didn't you listen." He stalks past the black priest, shoving my shoulder. "God, you don't ever fucking listen. And you sure as hell don't trust me."

I shove him back, my eyes glued to his face and not the naked torso, covered in scars and defined with muscle. "You haven't fucking earned it."

Rage flickers across his face, but I turn away before he can say anything.

"I can give you meds, Finn. You don't need Lori."

I jerk around, but Finn is laughing, a silent shaking of his shoulders. "No. No fucking way in hell."

Anger fills the priest's eyes, and his voice is tight and demanding, "Why not?"

Rage rips across his face, and I realize, really realize, how close Finn holds his emotions. How much he doesn't show, because now—here—I see it all. "Because you're a fucking traitor. I don't trust you Omar. I didn't then, and I don't now, and no matter how much time passes, no matter how many Order's you join and how far you climb, I never will. You can't undo what happened to Kelsey."

The other man is quiet, a large, brooding mountain. Finally, he nods. "Fine. I'll see you in my office in an hour."

Finn doesn't say anything as the black priest leaves with the quiet swish of his robes and soft snick of the door. He doesn't comment on the rumble of Omar's voice ordering his soldiers to escort us to him in an hour. He doesn't address that he's let more of his past slip, without telling me anything. He doesn't even look at me, just turns away and slams the bathroom door shut behind him.

Leaving me with the echoes of angry voices and more unanswered questions.

When we are ushered into Omar's office, the priest has changed into a pair of cargo fighting pants and a tight shirt that's still damp with sweat from his workout. There's a slim file on his desk that catches my attention. He gives us a brusque look as we enter and extends the file impatiently. Finn reaches for it, and Omar jerks it back. "Don't do this, O'Malley. You don't trust me, and I get that, but you know me. You know how far I'll go.

You don't know anything about Lori. She's ruthless and doesn't give a fuck about the Order."

Finn smirks. "Two things we have in common."

"If she takes the Stronghold, she'll kill us all. She doesn't believe it's the Firsts—she wants everyone born after the change slaughtered. Is that what you want to see happen? Is that what *she* would have wanted?"

Finn lashes out, faster than I can follow, and I see Omar's head snap back. The giant makes a low noise in the back of his throat and shakes his head hard. "Do not use her like that," Finn growls.

Omar stares at him hard, his face grim. "Get out. And god help us if she takes this Order from me." He tosses the folder and Finn catches it easily. He doesn't open it, just shoves it in a pocket and throws open the door. We're almost gone when Omar grabs his shoulder. "I'm here, O'Malley. If you need—"

"I don't," he says, interrupting Omar. Shutting him down without anything more than that. It's brutal, and I don't understand it. Finn tugs me against him, and I have one last glimpse of the giant black priest, his robes giving him a forbidding appearance, before Finn drags me away.

I stumble along behind him, past the soldiers lining the halls, and finally ask, "What now?"

"We give this to the Priestess. And we get the fuck out of here."

Chapter 9

Awkward Interludes

The truck feels like home. Strange, since the only time I've spent in it was driving to Vegas with a man I can't stand—but after twenty four hours, anything that *isn't* the Stronghold is a breath of fresh air. I slide into the passenger seat, my jeans rubbing against the sticky hot leather.

Finn cranks the engine and glances at me as he slams the door. I look past him, at the mountainous black priest. He's staring at Finn, his expression unreadable. I wait for Finn to acknowledge him, but he doesn't—he checks the safety on his Glock, drops it into the cup holder between us, and shoves the truck into gear. I look away from the priest as we lurch out of the underground parking garage and into the blinding Vegas sun.

We travel in silence for almost an hour before I finally look over at him. "What did he give you?"

Finn shrugs. "Its Order business, Nurrin. I don't get involved."

"You didn't tell him about the falling Havens."

It's not an accusation—more a quiet observation. It still makes Finn's lips twitch in irritation. "Do you really think I'd do anything to preserve the Order? I'd sooner let the zombies win."

It's a common sentiment against the Order. There was one unwritten rule of our changed world—don't kill the uninfected.

The Order didn't believe in that, and many wanted them dead because of it.

"Want to tell me what was going on between you and the priest?" I ask, staring out at the open land. It's spotted with trees and broken roadways, a few infects darting along the sand in the distance.

He doesn't answer—not that I thought he would. "You did well in there," he says instead.

I snap around to stare at him, so fast my neck pops. He smiles, a tiny twitch of his lips that I'm beginning to pick up on. "Did you just compliment me?"

"Don't act so surprised, Nurrin. I can see someone's assets."

His gaze flicks down briefly before it slides forward again, but I feel the touch of it like a hot brand on my breasts, stroking over my nipples. I flush and stare out the window, ignoring him and the soft, mocking laugh that echoes through the truck.

Chapter 10

Complications

It's the screams that wake me. I don't know how long I've been sleeping—only know my eyes feel gritty and the sun is high above us when I blink awake, the ghastly scream echoing in my ears.

The first thing that really sinks in is that we're not moving. The truck sits utterly silent—the engine isn't even ticking with heat anymore. I shiver in the silence as the scream comes again, and look over at Finn.

His hair is wet, his clothes sticking to him.

That's the second thing that sinks in. The scent of bleach and disinfectant is almost choking me, burning the inside of my nose as the fumes fill the truck.

I open my mouth, and Finn shakes his head, sharply. Scribbles something on the paper he's holding and hands it to me.

Outside.

I look out and a scream rises in my throat. His hand clamps down over my mouth, and I bite, anything to let off some of the terror. He doesn't flinch. The whimper that slips from my throat is barely a breath, unnaturally loud in the deathly quiet of the truck. He arches an eyebrow, and I nod tightly. Only then does Finn ease back, releasing his grip on me. I take a quiet breath and stare out the window.

The horde is massive. Larger than any I've ever seen. In Hellspawn, the largest horde we would get was between seventy and a hundred zombies. This is ten times that size. They move together with eerie precision, loping along, fingers clutching and releasing rocks as they go. Occasionally, one will scream and another will answer with a snarl, shoving the screamer out of the way as they dart through the desert. A few hesitate around the truck, sniffing and snapping at it. One catches on the razor wire and screams furiously before he rips himself free, leaving a chunk of rotted thigh behind.

They stream around us, moving like a river of death, and for the most part, don't even realize we're here. I shudder, staring at the dead faces, the vacant eyes. Every instinct screams to run, to find somewhere they can't reach me. Every instinct says that sitting like this is paramount to death.

I've learned to listen to my instincts—my instincts and my brother have kept me alive for twenty years. But this—Finn is still and silent, his eyes tracking the herd as it parts and sways and shakes the truck.

We sit there for what seems like forever, until finally—finally—they are gone, the last one darting past in a blur of decay and blood.

Even then, we don't move. We sit in utter silence until the herd vanishes completely, the sun glaring in our eyes. I can't feel my fingers, and somehow, I realize I've grabbed my gun. Finn's crossbow is sitting in his lap.

The sun begins to set, and I finally look at him. He's staring at nothing, his eyes half closed. He looks exhausted—worse than I've ever seen.

"When is the last time you slept?" I ask.

He shrugs, exhaustion pulling at him. "It's hard to sleep when there's no one watching your back."

That burns a little. "You can't keep me safe if you're dead from exhaustion," I say, sitting back. "And I would stand guard."

Finn's gaze snaps to me, startled. I don't say anything, and he's quiet for a moment, watching me. Finally, he cranks the engine. I wince at the sudden roar of noise, and he gives me that quirk of a smile that drives me fucking insane. But something is different, this time—almost like he's got a new-found respect that I haven't seen in him before.

It's full dark when we finally limp into Haven 18. The Wall gleams in the moonlight around us, the crack of a shot gun echoing across the mountains.

Finn is still driving, although I'm not sure how he's managed to keep awake. He stops the truck near the gate, and we wait as we're cleared. They take a little longer than usual—probably waking some poor medic—until Finn is cursing, his fingers drumming impatiently on the steering wheel. Finally, the medic arrives and the blood tests are done. Not terribly surprising, we're cleared clean and we drive through the gates. Immediately, Finn slams the truck into park and slides out. I scramble to follow him, grabbing my bag.

"We hit a horde about half way here. Looked like they were headed for Haven 22. You might want to send them word, that it's coming."

One of the Walkers sneers, and Finn rolls his eyes. "Or don't. Frankly, I don't give a fuck what you do. The truck needs to go through decontamination. Send it to Jesse—he knows how I like things done."

"We're not your servants, O'Malley. 18 isn't beholden to you or Haven 1."

Finn doesn't bother to answer the man, just turns and stalks into the night. I could question the soldier, but I don't—I follow Finn into the dark streets. We walk quietly, some of the tension draining from me. I can hear people talking, laughing in their homes, the lights dim for the night, but life clearly being lived. It makes me nostalgic—I want to be home, surrounded by Dustin and Collin, Kelly a quiet counterpoint. But I'm not. Kelly is dead, and Collin could be—Dustin could kill him. Home is gone, and I'm with Finn O'Malley, of all people.

"It's amazing, how secure and safe they think they are," he murmurs. I look at him, but Finn isn't talking to me. He's almost swaying with exhaustion.

We reach the house, and it feels comfortable, familiar. Without talking to me, Finn locks the doors behind us and stalks to his room. I hear the lock click into place, the creak of his bed, and the clank of his gun landing somewhere.

I sit on the couch and try not to think about how I came to be guarding Finn while he sleeps.

Chapter 11

Neutral Ground

I stare at the door, a knife in my hand. It's been quiet for a few seconds but—

BANG BANG BANG

Like clockwork, the pounding comes again. I should just answer the damn thing. Clearly my "ignore and hope it goes away" method is striking out.

Finn would be furious if I opened the door to a stranger. And in this Haven, the only person who isn't a stranger is Jesse, and he only just barely qualifies as more than that. He'd say it's too dangerous.

The banging comes again, and my fingers twitch on the knife, reflexively.

He can say it's too dangerous all he wants. The bastard's been sleeping for almost twelve hours straight, and this banging is gonna kill my nerves. A noise from the back of the house startles me. Finn stalks from his room, his hair a mess, drawstring pants riding low on his narrow hips. I look away, uncomfortable. I hate when he uses his body as a distraction. It's not fighting fair.

He ignores me completely, going straight to the door and yanking it open. "What the *fuck* do you want?" he snarls. I flinch back from the barely checked violence in his tone—it's the voice you hear before he kills someone.

The man on the other side of the door stares back impassively. He's shrouded in a light gray robe, the cowl pulled up and over his head. He looks like death—or what people imagined death to be, before the end of the world and the zombies came back.

"Priestess will see you now," he says.

Finn bares his teeth in a parody of a smile. "Your damn priestess will see me when I'm good and fucking ready."

He slams the door without letting the priest respond and heads back to his room.

"Get dressed," he snaps and slams the door behind him.

By the time we are dressed and get to the Order's club, we're both in a foul mood. Finn and I are escorted through the empty club, past the wheels and chains of the vice club. The scent of blood and sweat still hangs in the air, their own perfume.

Lori looks like she hasn't moved since we left. Her red robes pool around her as she perches on the desk, her black guard silent at her back.

She watches us with quiet intensity as Finn paces into the room and scowls. "What the hell, Lori. What the fuck do you think to accomplish by dragging me from my house? I have your damn information."

He throws the file at her, and the guard shifts, agitated. A slim hand lifts to still him before she plucks the file open and lazily glances over it.

"Very good, O'Malley," she almost purrs.

"You knew he'd be there—that Omar would work with me," Finn accuses without heat. She shrugs, delicately. "You manipulated me," Finn says, and I finally understand his anger.

"I did."

"I've killed for less, Priestess," he says, almost conversationally. A smile, amused, turns her lips up.

"I know. But I have what you want—meds. I gambled and won." She snaps her fingers, and the gray priest behind us disappears. "He'll bring the medicine. Now, give me the information about the zombies."

He stares at her, and the priestess smiles, a cool expression. I want to hate her, but it's damn hard—she's done what I didn't think anyone could: manipulate Finn. I admire that.

But I would hate to be the red priestess, when Finn no longer has use for her.

Chapter 12

A New Direction

Three shiny glass vials, filled with a viscous gold fluid. Two tubes of pills large enough to make me gag.

They sit on the counter like precious gold. I want to cry at the sight of them.

There isn't a cure to ERI-Milan. After the zombies rose, there was a backlash to medicine—even the most medicine-proponent person was hesitant to take something unnatural. The end of the world had a way of leaving a bad taste in ones mouth.

But eventually, even that fear faded. The most extraordinary thing about humans is we can overlook anything. Sure, it was the side effects of experimental drugs that triggered the apocalypse, but when drugs were good for keeping depression and anxiety and headaches at bay, what's a minor apocalypse? Humanity didn't die when ERI-Milan swept the earth, and eventually, the medical powers—CDC, WHO, drug companies, even Sanelos, began looking for the magical cure to ERI.

The problem was, they couldn't trace how it changed. When the zombie horde hit the Army troops, it triggered a change in the structure of the disease. That's what people didn't realize—not then, not even now. ERI wasn't a chemical suppressant. It was a disease that crippled the emotional response centers.

And diseases are living things. When it looked out the eyes of the horde in Atlanta, it saw its own destruction, and it did what any living thing is wont to do—it changed. It did whatever was necessary to survive.

There was no way to study it, though. And without studying the disease, it was virtually impossible to destroy it.

So the drug companies turned to lesser "cures." They came up with serums and neural inhibitors—risky medications that could stop a contact infection—sometimes.

It wasn't a cure, but it was almost better. The drug companies colluded in their labs and bottled hope. In a world without that, they created a drug that offered a chance, and sold it at a premium price.

Finn comes up beside me, jerking me from my thoughts as he scoops up the meds and tucks them into a secure pocket of his bag.

"Ready?"

I nod. I am so beyond ready to be done with this Haven and back with my brother. I grab my bag and follow him out of the house. He tosses his stuff into the back seat, and I settle on the passenger side, my gun and knife propped in the custom holster hanging from the door.

They stop us at the front gate. A man Finn's age approaches his window and leans in. "Sorry, sir. Walls are closed."

Finn gives him a disbelieving look. "Why?"

"Aldermen's orders. No one is allowed out, on account of a horde spotted headed this way."

For a heartbeat, I can't breath. I'm back in Hellspawn, the alarms screaming in my ears, the sound of zombies feasting a horrific counterpart. I'm in the silent truck, my heart pounding as hundreds of zombies whip past us, driven by hunger and some unknown *need*.

I shiver in my seat, the burning desire to escape slamming into me. "Finn," I start, and he nods, cutting me off.

"I know, Nurrin. We need to get out."

Chapter 13

Haven's Aldermen

It's impressive—and a little alarming—how quickly Finn can gather the Aldermen. The Haven has been closed, there are quite literally zombies at the gates, and Finn does nothing more than call Lissel. Within an hour, all of them are assembled, waiting a little impatiently as Finn and I enter the little room we first met Lissel in. She's sitting with five others—four men and a tired looking young woman.

"What do you want, O'Malley? We have better things to do then waste our time on you." One of the men, a thin, pointy faced man, gripes.

Finn ignores him, drops lazily into a seat. He kicks a chair out and nods at it—my invitation to sit. "I need out of the Haven."

"Can't help you. The Haven is closed until the horde passes or reinforcements arrive."

Finn is quiet, staring at nothing, for long enough that the aldermen begin to fidget. Finally, "Do you think holding me here will bring those reinforcements? I hate to break it to you, but Haven 1 forgot about me. They don't care about me or 18 or anything but their own survival. We're on our own here."

"You can bring people in." The alderman is older, with salt-and-pepper hair and the stiff demeanor of a war veteran.

"General Reid. You don't really believe that," Finn says, stretching lazily. "They sent you here to get rid of you after the war—if they'd forget one of their decorated veterans, why not me?"

"Because you were always more than a veteran, decorated or not. Reach out. Use your name, son."

Finn drops his feet to the ground and leans forward. "You aren't listening. They don't care. Most of the ones left in 1 don't even know I'm alive, much less who I am. They aren't coming to help you, and they aren't coming to help me. Even if I thought they would, I won't call for support. You have two options: wait for the horde and get ready to die, or get the fuck out of the Haven."

"Those aren't options," the quiet woman, Melinda, says.

"They're all you've got. I've seen it happen—I was in 8 when fell. You won't survive. Look around. Reach out to the Havens around you. Who haven't you heard from? Why do you think they're quiet? It's not because it's harvest time. It's because they're gone. The Havens are falling, and you have to wake up and face that."

"We can't leave," she says again, and her voice is a little desperate.

"Then get ready to die. Because the horde will come. And the Haven will fall. I'm leaving—you have no legal right to detain me here if I'm willing to take my chances in the Wide Open."

He nods at me as he stands, and I start for the door. My heart is pounding, crazily. Who *is* he?

"You can't just desert us," Lissel says, catching Finn's arm.

He whips around, shaking her off violently. "I can. I will. I warned you, I told you this was happening, and you ignored me. Do something or don't, but I won't sit here and die with you because you're too fucking stupid to get out of a sinking ship."

"Will you look? Look at the Haven and tell us we should evacuate!"

It's the younger woman, and something about her voice makes me hesitate. Finn grips my arm. "Keep walking, Nurrin. This isn't our problem."

It's not. My only concern should be for Dustin and Collin.

But there is something desperate about her, something in her eyes that makes me pause—a pleading.

I look at Finn. See the fury in his eyes and make my decision. Somehow, it doesn't feel as good as it used to, when doing something just because he didn't approve was almost a game.

It's still the right thing to do.

I turn away from him and the medicine that will save Collin and Dustin, and face the young Alderman. "You have thirty minutes. Show me."

Relief flashes across her face.

On the surface, 18 is like any other Haven. The majority of it is crop land. A few factories stand near the South wall. Shops line Main Street. Three massive stone structures comprise the Hives— sixty percent of the civilian population is packed into them.

On the surface, there is nothing different here. People walk to work at a snail's pace. Women chatter over laundry lines. Dogs bark in someone's house, and a man's voice echoes in song. It feels warm, cozy. Like home should feel.

It's a fucking illusion. There is nothing safe but a gun and someone you trust at your back. Even that isn't truly safe—safety is a luxury that died on an afternoon car ride with Emilie Milan.

Melinda drives us past the Hives and homes, shops and factories. To the very edge of the Haven, where the Wall backs up against the mountain face. There are more guards here then I expect. I glance at her, and she ducks her head, almost as if she doesn't want to admit to something. It doesn't bode well for whatever she's planning to show me.

"We have to walk from here," she says. Finn is silent, a seething presence behind me.

I try to ignore him and focus on the tunnel she leads us to. It's narrow, with a low ceiling. Three heavily armed guards are standing by the entrance, and Melinda flashes us an apologetic smile. "You need to verify your infection status."

I blink, startled. It's normal after traveling through the Wide Open, but we haven't been exposed since arriving in 18. She doesn't back down, though. Reluctantly I offer up my hand. The test is high quality, a cuff that wraps around my bicep and bites down with over a dozen needles. I yelp and Finn shifts restlessly.

After a few minutes, the needles retract and the cuff releases me. Finn goes through the same test—what surprises me is that Melinda does as well. There is a ring of red skin on her arm that tells me how often she comes here—and that every time she goes through a test this intense.

"The tunnel is narrow on purpose. I hope you aren't claustrophobic," Melinda says, ducking into the tiny opening. I glance back at Finn; he stares at me, expressionless.

The tunnel is long and winding, and just when I think I will scream from the pressure of the rocks above and around me, it tightens and we reach a guard with a drawn AK47. He eyes us, his expression lightening just a little when he sees Melinda.

Then he reaches for a small box on the side wall and hits it. A few seconds later, a series of lights flash, and the AK47 drops.

"You're clear. Go on in."

We take a step out of the cramped tunnel into a small cave. The walls are smooth, arching away and above us.

"What was that box?" Finn asks.

Melinda looks nervous, but says, "The siren alarm system. We modified it a little."

"Tampering with a Haven's alarm system is a federal offense."

"When Haven 1 bothers to check on us, they can drag me to jail," the alderman drawls. "In the meantime, I'm doing what's needed to keep my people alive."

"How?" I ask.

Melinda smiles and leads us into a man-made tunnel. We walk, and I'm silent, staring at the little caves that branch off. There's room after room of private residence, a large square filled with weapons, an entire wing of medics and kitchens. They all spiral inward, into a tightened grid of rooms protected by more soldiers.

"What is this?" I ask, needing to hear it.

"It's the world's biggest Hale Hall. It's what we can fall back to, if there is ever a massive breech. It's where we keep our children to keep them safe."

"It's a massive tomb." Finn says, flatly.

She flushes. "It's the best chance we have."

"And what happens when you come out? When you run out of food and think it's safe and poke your happy little head out only to find you were wrong and the infects are still right there? What happens then? Hiding doesn't *work*."

"Fighting doesn't either," Melinda snaps, glaring at him.

"That's why you don't do either," he says, quietly. "You can't live in fear of the day the zombies batter down your door—that isn't living. You live in *spite* of that day. You live because everything in our screwed-up world says we can't and we shouldn't and *fuck them*." He looks around and shakes his head. "But this isn't living. Hiding in a hole is just a slow way to die."

He turns away from her, his gaze hitting mine. "I'm leaving, Nurrin. Come or don't. I'm done here."

Chapter 14

New Plans and Old Behaviors

I don't hesitate this time. Truth be told, there isn't even a choice to be made. Collin trusts Finn, and that means I do. I might hate him, might want to stab him with my knife more often than I want to stab an infect, but I trust that following him will take me home. To Collin.

We're halfway back to the house, and more importantly, the truck, when he slides a glance at me from the corner of his eye.

"How far will you go to get home?"

I blink, a little startled. "How far are you thinking?"

A smile twists his lips, and a shiver of dread snakes along my spine. It's never good when Finn looks like that. "We can get out. It's going to be a

317

little trickier, with the gates locked. But it can be done. It will probably take a little more than you're comfortable with."

I frown at him. "Are you taking me back to the kink club?"

He snorts. "Never."

I shrug and look forward, my shoulders relaxing a little. "Whatever you do, it can't be worse than that, right?"

Something glitters in his gaze, and I look away. "Be careful, little girl. You have no idea how bad it can be."

I ignore the chill that chases its way down my spine and start walking again. "So what do we need to do?"

He shrugs. "For now, nothing. Tomorrow, I need a little time."

Chapter 15

Visiting Friends

Finn is sleeping or gone when I slip out. I'm not surprised to find that there's fresh coffee and two slices of bacon and cheese on a piece of burnt toast.

Clearly, Finn's breakfast skills need work.

I grab the weird sandwich and coffee and head out. As I jog down the stairs, I hear the distinct sound of the door locking behind me. Through a sheer force of will, I resist the urge to look behind me. I don't know what game he's playing or why this is important. But I know his goal is to get out of 18, and I can totally get behind that.

The Haven is abnormally quiet. People are retreating as the horde gets closer. Last night, sirens rang every hour, a different note letting the citizens know how close the horde was and how long they had—we had. I glance at the napkin my sandwich was wrapped in and hope that noon won't be too late.

There's no answer when I knock on Jesse's door, but I can hear the distant clang of tools on metal and muttered cursing. I grin and head around the corner of the mechanic's shop. The back yard is a junkyard of dead cars, broken into pieces and sprawled across the land. Old tires and pans of sticky, black oil are stacked to one side, and there's a narrow, curving path amongst the car parts. I follow it, deeper into the jungle of mechanics, until I hit a wall of solid razor wire.

"Jesse?" I yell, and I hear a muffled thud.

"Ren?"

"Let me in!" I shout. I hear a few tools rattle around before the wall of bladed metal parts and I crawl through.

Jesse is smudged with dirt and oil, his hair covered by a ratty bandana, and he looks startled—and a little bit nervous to see me. "What are you doing here?"

"We can't leave the Haven, and Finn is driving me crazy," I say glibly, "so I thought I'd visit the one friend I have in the Haven. Do you mind?"

He grins. "Not if you don't mind me working."

I look at the motorcycle. It's a little crotch rocket, like the one we rode out of Hellspawn on, and I cock my head at it. "Who is it for?"

"O'Malley. The Porsche financed this, so I'm getting it ready for him."

"What does that mean, exactly?"

"Upgrades on the tires, holsters for his guns and crossbow, zombie repellent leg guards and shatter proof wind shield. I'm adding bags made of zom armor, and a wraparound shield for whoever rides bitch."

I blink, staring at the unassuming little bike. "Something that little can handle that much weight?" I ask doubtfully.

"I reinforced her structure. And redistributed the gas tank, so she can go longer distances. She won't be as nimble as his last bike, and she might be a little exhausting to handle, but she'll do. And it's a helluva lot safer than the last bike. That was suicide on wheels."

An accurate description. Not that this will do a damn bit of good if we hit a horde like the one on the way back from Vegas.

"How long have you known Finn?" I ask.

Jesse hesitates for a heartbeat, long enough that I know he shouldn't be talking to me. But Finn sent me here, after all. He had to know I'd ask questions he would rather I didn't.

Too damn bad. I'll take whatever information I can pry out of Jesse.

"Since he was about twenty. He left the war before it was over. Went to Haven 1 to see what he could do there. But he made enemies. Finn isn't the most patient man in the world, and he was younger then, impetuous. He was a decorated war veteran, but he was also making serious demands—and at the time, no one wanted to hear from a sixteen-year-old that we should abandon the East. And he didn't have the protection of his father anymore. So after a while, he left. The president gave him free passage to wherever he wanted to go. He headed west. Took him a year or so to figure out where he wanted to be—I met him when he landed here briefly. But whatever Finn was looking for, it wasn't here. About a year after that, I heard he settled in 8."

I'm stuck on something he said earlier—not that he was in multiple Havens before he landed in Hellspawn. "Pass me that wrench?" he asks. I look blankly at the pile of tools, but can't see them. I can't think. Something warm and rough touches my face, and I jerk, startled.

"Hey," Jesse murmurs, softly. "What's going on in that pretty head, Ren?"

His lips are soft and full—I noticed that the first day I met him. Full and utterly kissable. And it could take my mind off Finn, off whatever he's hiding from me. I lean forward and catch them with my own. For a second, Jesse is still, startled. But then his hands come around me, pull me tight to him, his lips moving against mine. He nibbles at my bottom lip, almost a tickle, and I shiver. I want to feel more than I do. I deepen the kiss, licking at his lips and into his mouth, teasing over his teeth, a soft thrust and retreat.

Nothing. Absolutely fucking nothing.

I pull away, and I almost apologize. Jesse touches his lips, staring at me with surprise in his eyes. "Wow," he says softly.

I look away. "Yeah."

Chapter 16

Reflections and Interruptions

It's awkward, sitting with him, when I can feel his eyes on me, the hunger in them no longer hidden. But I do, because Finn made it clear when he needed me to return. He talks about cars, and I pretend to be interested; I talk about Dustin, and he pretends he isn't jealous. It works nicely for the both of us, honestly. My nerves are stretched tight when it's finally time to leave, an anxious thrumming that makes my knee jerk.

"I should go," I say, finally, standing.

Jesse stands with me, watching me with curious eyes. "You don't like Finn."

I shrug. "He's been part of my life for a long time, not that I ever really understood him. But no, honestly. I don't *like* him. He's annoying as hell, and he drives me fucking crazy—he refuses to answer any questions, yet he demands that I trust him, even when what he's suggesting is completely crazy."

"Like right now? You being here?"

I stop short and stare at Jesse. A smile quirks his lips up, but he doesn't seem pissed.

"You should go, Ren. Finn is waiting."

I nod awkwardly and go on tiptoes to kiss his cheek. "You aren't a bad guy, Jesse."

He laughs quietly at that as he pulls aside the razor wire and I slip out.

I find the priest a few blocks from Jesse's garage, but not close to Finn. I hesitate in the street, and two more in gray robes drift up behind me. Taking a deep breath, I force myself to walk forward. "What does she want?" I ask the giant bodyguard.

He doesn't say anything, just turns and glides down the sidewalk. I want to bolt—want to race back to the relative safety of Finn's home. Instead,

I grit my teeth and follow the priests of the Blessed Order.

Lori is a few streets over, sitting on the sidewalk, with her robes billowed out around her. Even on the dirty street, she looks like a perfectly made-up doll, a tiny porcelain creature with flawless features and impossibly perfect hair.

"Sit with me, pretty girl."

"I like standing," I answer, and her teeth flash in her tiny face. It's not a smile. Gritting my teeth, I lower myself down next to her.

"Tell me. Do you think he's right? That the zombies are adapting and searching for new food—that they are deliberately targeting the West, trying to isolate us as they did in the East?"

I shrug. "I don't know. Giving the zombies thought and cunning seems a little far-fetched and reaching. But Finn believes it, and my brother agrees. I trust my brother. I suppose that's where I stand."

"But you aren't doing anything to help Haven 18."

"What you do to survive is no one's business but your own. We have our own priorities," I snap shortly.

The little priestess smiles, and this time, there is genuine amusement there. It's not a grimace or a threat. "That I do believe. Finn O'Malley has always had unusual priorities."

I sneer. "The Order hardly has the right to point fingers about odd values. You kill humans."

"We recreate the sacred days," she says with calm conviction.

That's what terrifies me about Lori. Not that she's of the Order—Omar didn't scare me and he is their High Priest. It's that she believes, where others don't. Omar is there for power—Lori's here for conviction.

I glance at my watch, pissed that it's already almost twelve thirty. Whatever he wanted, I'm late. I stand up and dust off my pants. "As much as I enjoy chatting, I have to go."

"Yes. Yes, I suppose you should. Tell him that I allowed it."

My blood runs cold, and I go still, staring at her. Lori's eyes gleam with madness. I shiver despite the heat. "What did you say?"

"I am letting you go. Because for whatever reason, O'Malley wants you. Remind him that he owes me—not the Order, but me—for my leniency. I will save you, as long as I can, for the sake of Finn's goodwill toward the Order."

I don't understand—it doesn't make sense. None of it does, but then nothing around Finn ever does. I scramble away from her, and the priests that surround us drift back, letting us past. Lori laughs, her voice chasing me down the street. "Tell him what I say. The Order has marked you, First!"

I break into a run.

Part 4

The Horde Without End

*

I wish I had seen it—the world before Day One. It sounds amazing.

Nurrin Sanders

**

We should have died. Some days, I wish we had.

Finn O'Malley

Chapter 1

Old Lovers

She's late. I can tell as I unlock the front door—the house feels empty and abandoned.

This seriously fucks up my plans. I open the door and step aside. Lissel glides in behind me, all sleek curves and *fuck me* smiles.

This isn't gonna go like I wanted. I miscalculated, and someone will get hurt.

"Where is your little friend?" Lissel asks. Her tone grates on my nerves. Makes me grind my teeth.

"She's none of your fucking business," I say.

Her eyebrows go up at that, but I'm kissing her before she complains. Her arms are around me, and I remember why I used to fuck her. She throws everything into the kiss with no

333

inhibitions or hesitation. In any other situation, I'd be in. I'd be kissing her back, ready for sex. As it is, I go through the motions, but my mind is somewhere else. Wondering where the hell Ren is.

If Lissel notices my inattention, she doesn't say. She just reaches for my belt, fumbling it open.

Shit, if I don't get this stopped soon, Ren'll be walking in on more than I expected her to. Although it'll do its job, and that's all it really matters at this point. All that I can let matter. She has my pants open, hand clutching my dick. I groan, my head falling back as she drops to her knees and takes me in her mouth. With her head bent, all I see is blonde hair and, for a moment—just a moment—I can forget that isn't right. Then the sensations overwhelm me, and I don't fucking care who it is. All that matters is that she doesn't stop. Fingers cup my balls, rolling them as she sucks me to the back of her throat. Somehow, I've clutched her hair and my fist, pulling her along. She moans, vibrations running along my dick.

With a curse, I pull her to her feet. Lissel laughs, wiping her mouth.

I need to slow this down. There needs to be some kind of delay, a way to wait for Ren. I whip around, pinning her against the wall and grabbing the bottom of her shirt. Her body jerks when I rip it, and her eyes are angry, but hungry. I yank on her bra, and her full breasts spill out.

She's moaning, whimpering and shifting against me as I pinch her nipples, kissing her neck. She jerks up her skirt and reaches for me.

Too fast, too fucking fast. She's got me in her hand, a tight hot fist stroking my dick, and I can feel her wet heat. I thrust, and she laughs as I slip along her folds. She shifts, just enough that I don't slide deep into her. I growl, remembering why I quit finding my way to her bed—she's too damn manipulative. Everything is a game to her.

I grab her hips, angle, and thrust into her. She screams, her body spasming around my dick as I fuck her.

Nazarea Andrews

Distantly, I know this is fucked up. I know I'm taking it too far. I know that this *wasn't* the plan. But that's distant—all I can focus on is the white hot pleasure running through my body, and Ren's voice, ringing in my ears as I thrust into Lissel. I'm chasing my own orgasm—fuck Lissel and what she wants, she got me here despite my resolve, I'm going to get everything I can out of it.

Her nails are digging into my back, and she's panting as one leg wraps around me, meeting every thrust. I slam into her, and she shrieks, clawing at my back as her body tightens around me. My release slams into me, and my head drops back as I let everything go and surrender to the pleasure.

When I can see and think, I realize Lissel is smiling, a smug expression that makes my blood boil in a completely different way. I drop her leg, and she slides down the wall, tugging her bra into place while I tuck my dick away. I take a deep breath and turn to look at Nurrin.

She's staring at us with an expression I don't think I've ever seen on her face—disgust and loathing and fury. I stare at her, my face blank, masking my fascination. Finally, she shakes herself and twists to look at me. "What the fuck are you doing?"

There's a dizzying rush of relief. She might be furious, but she's using that to play the emotions I need from her—she's using it to get us out.

"Scratching an itch," I say, pushing away from Lissel. "How was Jesse?"

Something flickers in her eyes that makes my blood run cold. I step toward her, and she skitters back a step. *Fuck.* Maybe I wasn't the only one with screwed-up plans. "Did you fuck him?" I ask, my voice low.

Her gaze darts to mine, disbelieving. "Are you serious? You think you have a single inch to stand on?"

"Don't worry," Lissel purrs, approaching me on one side, "we're just old friends catching up."

Nurrin gives the alderman a disdainful look and sniffs. "Bitch, do you really think I care who he fucks? I just care that we're still trapped in this hell hole."

Lissel goes stiff, and I finally look at her. "That's true. Old friends, and all. Help me out, Lissel."

"Fuck you, O'Malley," she hisses, outraged.

Nurrin coughs, muttering, "You already did that." I shoot her a dirty look. Then I focus on Lissel.

"This doesn't have to be difficult, Lissel. Staying in 18 is going to be messy. Do you remember, what I told you about messy?"

A sliver of fear flickers in her eyes, and then she shakes her head, stubbornly. "I can't help you. I won't risk the Haven."

I make an impatient noise, and Lissel flinches. "It's not just you, you jackass," she snaps. "If it was, then I'd say fuck it and open the gates. But it's not—every time the gates open, we risk a breach. I can't authorize that, even if I wanted to."

"Every Haven has a back door," Ren says, her voice sharp and disbelieving. I know she's thinking about the tunnel we used to escape Hellspawn.

Lissel is shaking her head. "We sealed it."

"Why on earth would you do something that fucking stupid?" I demand, sharply.

"Because we have the Hale Hall. I know Melinda showed you, so you have to know we'll hide before we run."

I shake my head, furious. Look at Ren over Lissel's blonde hair. The alderman is waiting, almost impatiently watchful, for my next move.

I don't have a lot of options. "Get my bags."

She nods, and ducks into the back of the house. I reach behind me then lean into Lissel's space. "I didn't want to do it this way," I murmur.

"Finn, you need to accept this. Running won't work this time—and whatever that girl is dragging you out to, it's not worth it. You can survive here—even if your ties in Haven 1 have dried up, you have a place here. I'd make sure of it."

She doesn't get it. She never has. That's the problem—she wants to give me something that no one can. Stability and a place to belong, for fuck's sake. What does that even mean in a world like ours?

I stare at her and shake my head. Lean in to kiss her quickly, because I don't dislike Lissel. I just have priorities. And she isn't one.

Ren clears her throat, and I twist to look at her. She's got that foul expression again. "I need you to do one thing, Ren," I say, and she visibly flinches. She's not used to her nickname on my lips.

"What?" she asks warily, and I wish I could do something about that. I wish I could ease her distrust—but I can't, and my priority right now is to just get us out.

"Trust me?"

I wait, perfectly still, not even breathing. Behind me, Lissel is fidgeting, and in front of me, Nurrin is staring at me with her big green eyes.

Finally, she nods. Something tight and tense loosens in my chest, and I give her a grim smile.

Then I yank off a length of silver duct tape and wrap it quickly around Lissel's wrists.

"What the hell are you doing?" She shouts, jerking away. I yank her back, the tape cutting into her skin. Nurrin steps up, her gun in her hand. I give her a tiny nod, and the barrel of the gun presses into the soft skin of Lissel's throat, skin I so recently kissed.

I can't think like that. Not right now. I finish securing Lissel's hands, Nurrin's gun holding her steady. Then I stand up and stare at her. "Now. Here's what's going to happen—you are going to get us out of the Haven. And if you do it without any trouble, I'll let you go. If you don't—it'll make my life messy."

"You wouldn't dare kill me," she spits.

I smile, lazily. "You didn't think I'd fuck you and tie you up, either. Keep betting on what I don't have the balls to do."

Lissel's mouth snaps shut and I nod. "Good. Let's go."

I shove her into the back of the truck, and Ren slides in, her gun still pointing directly at Lissel's head. She glances at me curiously. "What's the plan?" she murmurs.

I arch an eyebrow, and she rolls her eyes. "Asking a question is *not* a lack of trust."

"Just wait," I mutter.

"You don't know, do you?" Ren asks, as horrified as she is amused.

She's wrong. I do know. It was the plan from the beginning.

The gate is sealed. Two dozen guards are milling around it, their weapons pointed at the ground as they talk to each and wait, bored, for the change of watch. I'm about to throw a kink into all of their plans.

I park the truck and stalk around the front. The soldiers surround me, almost instantly. "You need to clear out," a particularly brave one says. I glance at him, and the poor kid wilts, falling back a few steps. Until I drag their lovely Alderman out by her bound hands.

Then their guns snap up and train on me.

"Put those down," Lissel snaps, furious. "The idiot wants outside."

"The gates are sealed. No one in or out, sir. And abducting our alderman is punishable by quarantine."

"Or being put outside the Walls," I add. "Which you're welcome to do."

The soldiers look confused, and I take a deep breath. "Why are the Walls sealed?"

"Infection. We can't risk letting it inside," the guard says promptly.

I stab the needle deep into Lissel's arm, making my motions clear. You couldn't miss them if you were blind—and she screams, loud enough to wake the dead. Outside, the zombies scream in response.

I hear Ren's tiny gasp, but she doesn't do anything to step in. She doesn't scream at me to stop. "Let me out," I say, keeping my finger on the plunger. "Now. Or I'll infect her and you'll be facing a breach." The guards hesitate, and Lissel is hyperventilating in my arms, fighting tooth and nail to get away from me. I clamp an arm down over her throat until she sags against me. Look at the guards. "It's your choice."

The guards hesitate, and she screams, "Shoot the motherfucker. Now!"

"She's already been exposed," one guards says, quietly. That's all it takes—the whispers spread like wildfire. Within a few seconds, they're reaching for the gate lift. "You have to be quick," the captain orders.

I nod. "Nurrin. Take the wheel," I order. She's staring at me with wild, wide eyes. I tug Lissel into the truck, almost in my lap, and snarl, "Drive!"

She does. Lissel falls into me with a yelp, and I jerk the needle free. "Sit still."

"Fuck you," she snarls. I don't have time to pay attention because Nurrin shouts my name and we slam into the horde. The truck shudders as the razor wire slices through the undead. Blood and gore explode from the front of the truck. From all sides, bodies slam into us, the screams shaking the air.

"Get in the back, Lissel." I snap, reaching for my crossbow. "Nurrin. Keep her steady and moving. We're dead if we stop."

She nods, and from the corner of my eye, something slams down toward my temple. I move without thinking, my blade swinging up and cutting across Lissel's belly. Her eyes go wide, shocked. Ren screams, a shocked noise she chokes off almost immediately. The scent of blood fills the tiny cab. For a moment, there is only silence and the rasp of the dead outside. I curse and shove the little crawlspace open. The dead scream, furious at the scent of blood. "What the hell are you doing?" Nurrin shouts, more furious than scared.

"Saving our lives," I answer and grab Lissel's shoulders. Her hands are gripping me, causing me to stumble. Around me, the razor wire shakes as the zombies pummel it, and it occurs to me this is probably the stupidest thing I've done in forever.

Then I don't think. Nurrin guns the engine and I throw the body—it's only a body—out. Blood sprays in a glittering red arc, and the zombies whip around, following the scent of it. Nurrin slams the gas down, and we shoot away as the infects feast.

Chapter 2

The Hole

It's been hours. She's quiet—lost in her own thoughts—and I don't push. I don't want to see distrust in her eyes, or disgust, so I turn away.

I never turn away from the truth, but this time I do. There's no way to accept what I did. I can't ask her to—it's hardly a fair request.

The sun is dropping, and I glance at her. "Stop or keep going?"

Nurrin gives me a slightly startled look, like she forgot I was even here. We're in a deserted strip of the Wide Open, nothing but scraggly trees and sand to keep us company. "Keep going. We'll hit the Hole around midnight if we keep going."

I nod. "Want me to drive?"

She shakes her head, staring out the windshield. Her fingers tighten, briefly, on the wheel. "Why did you have the virus?" she blurts out. "How could you threaten someone with exposure like that?"

I don't answer for a few minutes, staring at the little vial, now neatly capped. Without letting myself hesitate, I stab it into my leg and decompress the plunger.

Nurrin hits the breaks so fast and hard, I'm thrown around. She falls out of the truck, and even before she's clear, the gun is trained on my head. Her whole body is shaking, but that's steady—the barrel doesn't waver at all.

I drop the needle and lift my hands, a gesture of surrender. "It's a saline solution," I say. Nurrin doesn't seem to register I spoke, so I repeat it, louder. "It's not the virus, Nurrin. It's a placebo. I just needed them to believe it was ERI-Milan."

"I believed it," she shouts.

"You trusted me enough to get in the truck. I swore to get you to your brother, Nurrin. I will. Don't doubt me now."

"You fucked her today!" she says, her voice shrill. "And then you killed her, fed her to the damn horde. How can you expect me to keep trusting you?"

Frustration boils in me, but I shake my head. Lean my head back. "You have to decide that, Ren. You can decide I did it because that's what it took to get you out of 18. Or you can decide I'm a monster. Eventually, you have to quit hiding behind your anger and make a decision." I throw the empty needle aside and slide into the driver's seat. "Now. Are you coming with me?"

Chapter 3

Discoveries

It's pitch black when we reach the Hole. I park the truck and lean over to shake Nurrin's shoulder a little. She blinks sleepily, and it's a struggle to force myself back to my side of the vehicle.

"We're here," I say. She nods and yawns.

There aren't any infects around—strangely, I haven't seen any in hours. But I'm not into taking unnecessary chances. "Got your stuff?" She nods, shrugging her bag onto her back.

"Can we go down in the dark?"

I hand her a flare stick. "Crack that when we get out. And move quick—we're alone for now, but you know how that goes."

She nods, and eagerness slips across her face. "Ready?" I ask, grabbing my knife.

We scramble out of the truck in perfect synchronization. She's at the side of the canyon, the pink flare sparkling at her side, and I nod at her. "Go." She doesn't wait or argue—apparently we have made progress since leaving. She edges down the cliff face as I glance around.

My blood runs cold as I take in the empty cliff. Something is wrong.

I push aside the sensation, the stomach-curdling fear, and follow Nurrin down the canyon.

Nurrin's pack is in the entry, and I step over it and her burning flare. Toss it and mine out over the cliff. They flare brilliant and bleeding as they plummet to the canyon floor. Behind me, Nurrin is moving around the little cave, lighting candles and calling Dustin's name.

I can taste the stale air. No one is here. No one has been here. Blood is on the ground, pooling on the low couch. It smells old and coppery. I close my eyes and face the open canyon, into the midnight sky, and listen as she gets more and more panicked. Until, finally, she's at my side, and I know how upset she is.

Nurrin doesn't cry. Not in front of me. She never has, not in the years I have known her brother. But tears are standing in her big eyes now, and her expression is furious and disbelieving. I draw her into my arms without thinking, and stare into the night as she buries her face in my chest and says, her voice muffled, "They aren't here. Collin is gone."

THE END.

Acknowledgements

As always, there are a host of people to thank.

First—my readers, who followed me from University of Branton to this crazy world I've imagined. I hope you enjoyed it as much as I did!

The Indie Ignites—gosh, you ladies are so awesome. Thanks for the cookies and talking me down from the ledges. I couldn't ask for a better group of friends and colleagues.

My family—Mom, for listening to me ramble, Lester and Kathy for not minding too much when I say at dinner 'I have a new book idea!' and my amazingly awesome sister in law and brother in law, for being amazingly awesome.

Thanks to my wonderful beta readers—Melissa, JC, Cameron, Heather and Felicia. Y'all have helped so much bringing this all together. Big hugs and lots of cookies for you all!

Pandora and I Heart Radio, which makes writing so much easier.

The Infects, who spread their excitement like good little zombies should.

My crazy awesome cover artist, who has made this book one of my prettiest. And also, something I could hang on my walls. (Don't judge me!) And my wonderful editor, Rachel Bateman, who amuses me with her notes, and keeps my em dash usage in check. You ladies make me so much better at this. And any mistakes in editing—those are all on me.

Chanteé. Dear gracious, you and Nathan deserve a whole paragraph. Thank you. Thank you thank you thank you. The videos and formatting and just general crazy amounts of support, not to mention handling the crazy texts—all of it makes you the best EVAH.

Bri—you have been Finn's longest standing, biggest fan. You rock, lady! *gentle tackle hugs*

My amazing publicist, Jessica. You don't even *like* zombies, but Finn converted you and the ideas you've had for this book have blown me away. I—and this book—would be lost without you.

Finally, always, my kids and Michael. For picking up the slack when I drop it when on deadline, to the patience when I'm 'one more minute, honey, Mommy's writing' to the sweet encouragement and excitement when you see my book and show your friends at school—you four are my world. I love you. ♥

About the Author

Nazarea loves zombies and creating romantic tension on the page and off comes naturally to her. So it was only a matter of time until her two passions combined.

Nazarea Andrews, is an avid reader and tends to write the stories she wants to read. She loves chocolate and coffee almost as much as she loves books, but not quite as much as she loves her kids. She lives in south Georgia with her husband, daughters, and overgrown dog

N~'s other work includes the super-sexy University of Branton series, a series of haunting dystopian romances based off of fairy tales, and she has recently co-authored a dangerously sexy Mafia romance. For more information on her work, please visit her website at www.NazareaAndrews.com.

Follow N~ on Facebook & Twitter today!

Prince of Blood and Steel

From Nazarea Andrews and AJ Elmore

The exiled heir has returned home....

Seth Morgan has returned to New York to find his family's crime syndicate in shambles and his brother plotting a coup. When a vicious retaliation puts Caleb in the ground, the younger prince is left to find his own answers in a family that feels like strangers.

A sheltered princess no one needs....

Emma Morgan has lived her life in the syndicate, protected and sheltered from their way of life. When her favorite cousin returns and asks for her loyalty, she doesn't hesitate—she's been loyal to Seth most of her life. But the further they dig into the mysteries surrounding Caleb's death, the more both are forced to realize that the most dangerous thing isn't the crime they broker—it's the family they've trusted.

Coming January 2014
Add Prince of Blood and Steel to your GoodReads List now!

www.ingramcontent.com/pod-product-compliance
Lightning Source LLC
Chambersburg PA
CBHW061925170626

46813CB00006B/2298